# The U-nique LOU FOX

# The
# U-nique
# LOU
# FOX

## Jodi Carmichael

pajamapress

**First published in Canada and the United States in 2022**

Text copyright © 2022 Jodi Carmichael
This edition copyright © 2022 Pajama Press Inc.
This is a first edition.
10 9 8 7 6 5 4 3 2 1

www.pajamapress.ca          info@pajamapress.ca

 Canada Council   Conseil des arts          ONTARIO ARTS COUNCIL
for the Arts      du Canada                 CONSEIL DES ARTS DE L'ONTARIO
                                            an Ontario government agency
                                            un organisme du gouvernement de l'Ontario

The publisher gratefully acknowledges the support of the Canada Council for the Arts and the Ontario Arts Council for its publishing program. We acknowledge the financial support of the Government of Canada through the Canada Book Fund (CBF) for our publishing activities.

**Library and Archives Canada Cataloguing in Publication**
Title: The u-nique Lou Fox / Jodi Carmichael.
Names: Carmichael, Jodi, author.
Description: First edition.
Identifiers: Canadiana 20210384697 | ISBN 9781772782585 (hardcover)
Classification: LCC PS8605.A7559 U55 2022 | DDC jC813/.6—dc23

**Publisher Cataloging-in-Publication Data (U.S.)**
Names: Carmichael, Jodi, author.
Title: The U-nique Lou Fox / Jodi Carmichael.
Description: Toronto, Ontario Canada : Pajama Press, 2022. | Summary: "Louisa, a fifth grader who has ADHD and dyslexia, wishes her overly tough teacher would disappear—then fears she has unleashed a curse when Mrs. Snyder becomes ill. Lou throws herself into the play she is writing and directing for her friends, but conflict follows when she becomes too pushy. At home, Lou alternates between jealousy and excitement as she prepares to become a big sister at last" -- Provided by publisher.
Identifiers: ISBN 978-1-77278-258-7 (hardcover)
Subjects: LCSH: Attention-deficit hyperactivity disorder – Juvenile fiction. | Teachers – Juvenile fictions. | Siblings – Juvenile fiction. | BISAC: JUVENILE FICTION / School & Education. | JUVENILE FICTION / Disabilities & Special Needs. | JUVENILE FICTION / Social Themes / Emotions & Feelings.
Classification: LCC PZ7.1C37Un |DDC  813.6 – dc23

Cover art and interior illustrations by Peggy Collins
Cover and book design—Lorena González Guillén

Set in 12-point Helvetica and 18-point/24-point OpenDyslexic with considerations for dyslexia-friendly design

Manufactured by Friesens
Printed in Canada

**Pajama Press Inc.**
11 Davies Avenue, Suite 103, Toronto, Ontario Canada, M4M 2A9

Distributed in Canada by UTP Distribution
5201 Dufferin Street Toronto, Ontario Canada, M3H 5T8

Distributed in the U.S. by Ingram Publisher Services
1 Ingram Blvd. La Vergne, TN 37086, USA

To my critique partners
Deborah Froese, Alice
Hemming, Louise Morriss,
and Candice Sareen.
Without you, Lou Fox
would not exist.

Sarah, Emma, and Drew:
you are my heart.

And finally, to my mom.
This one's for you!

—J.C.

Text design and font selection for
this book have been made with
consideration for readers with dyslexia.

The body text is set with Helvetica;
headers have been set with
OpenDyslexic.

An accessible EPUB format
is also available under the
ISBN 978-1-77278-259-2

# Table of Contents

# Chapter 1

# Three-Headed
# Fifth Grader

I have big plans. Huge plans. Boldly **au-da-cious**
plans.

In addition to being the youngest playwright in
history, I want to be the world's youngest Cirque
du Soleil gymnast. That means I must be as
rubbery as humanly possible. Even though I am
extremely bendy, I am not alone in my bendiness.
There are plenty of flexible kids out there. In
fact, my two best friends, Lexie and Nakessa,
are also **ex-ceed-ing-ly** bendable, which is why
we've called ourselves the Bendables since first

grade. Being surrounded by all this bendability is a constant reminder to practice my flips, splits, and tumbling whenever and wherever possible.

Every morning before the bell rings, Nakessa, Lexie, and I meet under the massive oak tree in the school field to take turns stretching out each other's legs. Just like every day, that's what we were doing the day everything began to change.

"Remember, Lexie," I said as a cool fall breeze blew my hair in every direction, "no matter what I say, do **not** let go." I tucked tangled strands behind my ears and pressed my back against the nubby tree bark, then I kicked my leg out straight.

"But what if you beg?" Lexie grabbed my ankle, slowly pushing my leg up toward my shoulder.

"Nope."

"What if you cry?" A gust of wind rained oak leaves down on us.

"Never."

"What if your face turns blue?" Nakessa asked, as she zipped up her navy puffer vest. She flung her black braids over her shoulders and began to sing. "*If Lou's face turns blue,*" she trilled, stretching her arms out wide, "*what will we dooooo?*"

Nakessa is forever making up songs. About everything. It's my number one favorite thing about her. My next favorite Nakessa thing is that she raids her dad's closet every morning.

Lexie laughed. "Nice song. I like the tune, but why would Lou's face turn blue?"

Nakessa shrugged. "Faces always turn blue in movies."

"This is **not** a movie," Lexie replied. She slowly pushed my leg up a few inches.

"Imagine if this was a movie. I would be a famous gymnast, dazzling the world with my moves," I said, beginning to feel real pain.

"At least if it was a movie there wouldn't be singing," Lexie said.

"Wrong." Nakessa crossed her arms. "There are plenty of movie musicals. What about *Annie*?" She burst into song again. "*The sun'll come out tomorrow!*"

"Bet your bottom dollar, she'll sing the whole song," Lexie finished.

Nakessa cartwheeled behind Lexie, her long legs poker straight. It was nearly as good as my cartwheels.

Another gust of wind blew. Shivering, Lexie propped my leg against her hip so she could pull up her jacket hood. Her pale face looked even tinier encircled by the gray fur trim.

"Blue faces...." I said, as Lexie pushed my leg up again. "Maybe we can add blue faces into our play!"

Lexie frowned. "If there are blue faces in

15

*The Haunting at Lakeside School*, I want magic. You already agreed to Nakessa's ghosts. I think I should be able to use my Harry Potter wand."

"Fine. Magic...is...in." My hamstrings burned. My heart began to pound.

Nakessa stopped cartwheeling and stepped closer. Her cheeks now flushed pink. "Your face is actually going bright red—like a fire engine."

"It's...okay...." I exhaled. My heartbeat boomed in my ears. "Don't...stop!" It was hard to speak.

"Are you sure? You're normally fish-belly pale." Lexie lowered my leg an inch.

"F-fish...belly?"

Lexie moved her face so close to mine our noses almost touched. "You're sweating across your nose. Your freckles are even sweating."

"No pain...no—"

The morning bell rang. Lexie dropped my leg.

I slumped against the tree and rubbed my thigh muscles. "Was my foot close to my ear?"

"Uhm...maybe a little closer than yesterday."

My whole body sagged.

*"Don't worry, Lou. We're here for...you!"* Nakessa sang as she linked an arm through mine.

"All for one and one for all!" Lexie took my other arm.

"Ready," I said.

"Steady," Lexie said.

# The U-nique Lou Fox

"*Freddy*," Nakessa sang.

"Go Bendables!" we cheered.

Then, like every morning, we ran across the field like a three-headed fifth-grader. With arms linked, we dodged around the other students.

And like every morning, my heart soared.

Why?

Because just before school was my favorite time of the day. I could still pretend the day ahead would be **spec-tac-u-lar**, which would be way better than the best. That was before I stepped a pinky toe into school and the reality of the place sank in, squashing my soul. Okay. Maybe a little dramatic, but if you were me, you'd find school soul-sucking too.

17

# Chapter 2

# Be Careful What You Wish For

**M**y gaze flew around the classroom, past the huge world map with font so small it was impossible for me to read, over the list of classroom rules we were supposed to have memorized, and stopped on our teacher's favorite poster. That I **had** memorized, because Mrs. Snyder had said the words nearly every day at the beginning of September: Life is all About Making Mistakes and Learning From Them. I'm a pro at making mistakes. Learning from them, not so much. Mrs. Snyder said it's supposed to encourage us. I don't need any encouragement when it comes to making mistakes.

"I'm pleased with almost everyone's scores," Mrs. Snyder said as she placed my spelling test face down on my desk. "Some of you will have to work harder." My heart cannon-balled into my stomach.

Hmmm. Who could Mrs. Snyder possibly be talking about?

Hint One: "Some of us" was a **she**.

Hint Two: **She** was astoundingly bendy.

Hint Three: **She** planned to be a famous Broadway playwright.

I glared at Mrs. Snyder's slightly rounded back as she continued up the aisle. I wanted to growl at her, but that's way too grade one-ish. No one growls in fifth grade.

"I'd like you to review the words you misspelled. Spelling can be tricky, but practice makes better," Mrs. Snyder said, standing in front of the whiteboard next to her desk.

I groaned.

Although **growling** and **groaning** are very similar sounds, they're not identical. They're like fraternal siblings. Similar, but different. And groaning is one hundred percent acceptable in fifth grade. I mastered it in fourth.

That's also when I determined that I hate

English class—especially on spelling test days.
And I triple-hate test result days.

I scowled at my paper. Stupid spelling.
I already knew I'd bombed the test. It's my
MO—*Modus Operandi*. Dad says that's Latin
for the way someone does something. For
me, the way I do spelling is by failing.

"*Pssst*, Lou. Give one to Nakessa." Lexie
reached across the aisle to pass me two Love
Hearts. I passed a purple **Cutie Pie** heart over my
shoulder to Nakessa, who sat right behind me.

I kept the orange heart. My favorite. I glanced
at the words. **Be Mine**. Those I could read.
I popped the candy into my mouth. The tangy
sweetness zinged on my tongue.

"Yum, yum, yum," Nakessa murmured behind
me.

Nakessa's MO is always to be tons of fun, that
and to sing about…anything.

Lexie's MO is to be stellar at everything
academic. She's academically gifted. That would
be annoying, except she's also a stellar friend.

And Lexie always has the best candy. Like,
always. In fact, today she said she had a surprise
for us. Candy her mom had brought back from
her latest business trip to England. I knew Lexie
could've eaten this surprise candy herself, and
we'd never have known. But that's not a Lexie

Chan thing to do. She's a do-unto-others kind of person. Lexie was saving this English candy to share for recess.

Best friends like the Bendables are hard to find.

Nakessa poked me in the back with a pencil. "How'd you do on the test?"

I rolled my eyes. Best friends like the Bendables are nearly as hard to find as a C on a spelling test for me. If I were the superhero Wolverine, spelling would be my lake or ocean. Wolverine drowns in water, I drown in the alphabet. Spelling is my biggest challenge, but to be honest, school in general is not one of my strengths. That's not a huge secret. I like math only slightly better than English, and don't get me started on social studies. Too much reading. Thankfully there's art. I adore art.

"So, what'd you get?" Nakessa whispered.

I forgot she'd asked the question. I shrugged. "I'm a hundred percent sure I flunked," I whispered back. "I wish it was different, but as my Grammers says, 'Wishing for something that can't be is like a hound dog wishing to fly like an eagle. It's for fools who can't accept the truth.'" I used my best Grammers' South Carolina accent, which was hard to do with a Love Heart in my mouth.

Nakessa giggled. She always cracks up when I speak like my grandmother. Too bad Dad didn't have the same accent. Or me. I'd love to talk "Southern" all day long.

"But then Grammers also says, 'Be careful what you wish for, because it might come true.'" I switched back to everyday Lou. "I've been wishing school didn't exist for forever, but here we are sitting in—"

"Ah-ah. No talking please," Mrs. Snyder said.

I jumped in my seat, crunching down on what remained of my candy. Somehow our teacher had crossed the room without my noticing. She was crazy stealthy for an old lady. I squinted at her. "Tell me the truth, Ma'am," I said drawling my words, South-Carolina style. "Are you part Shadow Phantom?" I'd read about those evil villains in one of Dad's old comic books.

Everyone around us giggled hard.

"That's enough class!" Mrs. Snyder frowned, sending dozens of new wrinkles across her crinkled forehead. Next time I needed an evil villain in a play, I was totally adding one with monstrous wrinkles. A cackling witch with bulging veins and bloodshot eyes emerged in my mind—

"No more nonsense, Louisa," Mrs. Snyder snapped, interrupting my witch-villain daydream. She paused dramatically, which she loves to do. Shadow Phantoms must like to watch their victims squirm. She stared at me over the top of her black-rimmed glasses. "The truth is, you need to pay less attention to making jokes and more attention to your work."

The truth is, if you looked in the dictionary under the words **academically challenged**, you would see the name Louisa. And then in those slanty letters that are supposed to tell you how to actually say the word: \*Loo-ee-zah*\.

Those slanty letters only help if you have a basic grasp of every sound in the English language. If you don't—like me—they are useless \*Yu-sss-less*\. Like me at school.

"*Psst,*" Lexie whispered as Mrs. Snyder silently stepped down the aisle. "Don't change Loubadoo. I like you just the way you are."

Easy for Lexie to say. She and Nakessa were perfect. But even with the Bendables on my side, it didn't change one simple, but important fact. The Shadow Phantom didn't like anything about me. Never had and never would.

# Chapter 3

# Frus-trat-ing

Causing annoyance or upset
because of an inability to change
or achieve something.

**M**rs. Snyder stooped over Little Jack's desk
in the front row, chatting quietly with him. He's
an ace at math. Ever since first grade, we've
had two Jacks in our class. Little Jack isn't
nicknamed Little Jack just because the other
Jack—Big Jack—is huge. Little Jack got his
nickname because his birthday's after Big Jack's.

I flipped over my test. Four out of ten. Not the
worst I've done. Everyone was busily printing
out the words they'd missed. I glanced out the
window. Puffy, whipped-cream clouds floated

across the blue sky. Our oak tree swayed in the breeze. I closed my eyes. I swear I felt that breeze on my face.

My eyes popped open to glance up at the clock. Six minutes until the recess bell. Forever. I doodled my name all over my paper.

## Louisa Elizabeth Fitzhenry-O'Shaughnessy

A thirty-six-letter name is a curse for someone who can't spell and finds reading next to impossible. Being dyslexic is no joke. Nor is the word **dyslexic** for someone who is.

I looked back at our oak tree. I should **not** have done that. That was the day's first mistake. I should have kept my eyes firmly on my paper, but when I begin to wonder about something, it's almost impossible to stop my brain from drifting away. And when I stared at our tree, I began to wonder if I could climb it to the very top. Even though I'm exceedingly athletic, I'd still need help. Nakessa's way taller than me. She could boost me up, lickety-split. I smiled as I drifted into my imagination. I could see Nakessa swooping her thick braids up into a floppy bun. Imaginary me stepped into her cupped hands. We wobbled around a bunch, laughing. Imaginary

Lexie marched over and made us take deep breaths and focus. Once Nakessa and I were steady, I leapt into the air, backflipping—

"Louisa, can you hear me?" Mrs. Snyder's nasally voice interrupted my backflip. Instead of grabbing the next tree limb, imaginary me landed in a heap. Then in a poof, the three imaginary Bendables disappeared.

I blinked and blinked again. Mrs. Snyder was right in front of my desk. Even by Shadow Phantom standards, she was impressively stealthy.

"Yes, Mrs. Snyder," I replied. "I can hear you." Heat rushed up my neck. It wasn't a lie—technically. I could **hear** her, but I knew that's not what she meant. This wasn't the first time I'd daydreamed in class. If being dyslexic was my superpower, having ADHD on top of that made me a mega-superhero.

"What did I just say?" Mrs. Snyder crossed her arms and peered at me over her glasses again. She didn't blink, which was unnerving. Probably part of her Shadow Phantom training.

"Uhm..." I glanced over at Lexie.

Lexie's gaze flashed to my paper and back up.

"My test," I said. "You want me to...look...at it?"

Mrs. Snyder sighed. "Yes, Louisa. In fact, I'd like you to look at it during recess."

"Wh-what?" I dragged my eyeballs away from

Mrs. Snyder and over to Lexie. "Not recess."

Lexie's brown eyes locked on me.

"But-but Lexie and Nakessa...we're working on our new play, *The Haunting at Lakeside School*. It's going to be—"

**Brrrriiinng!**

Saved by the bell! I pushed away from my desk.

"No, Louisa. Sit back down." Shadow Phantom turned her back to me and faced the rest of the class. "All right, grade five. Before you race outside, I need to remind you of the upcoming talent show. It's in less than two weeks. The sign-up sheets are still on the bulletin board outside the gym. Spots are filling fast, so if you want to take part, don't leave it any longer." She pulled a tissue from her pocket and dabbed at her forehead. "Okay! Time for recess. Please remember only grades three and four on the play structure today."

Like a plucked dandelion, I wilted onto my desk. My cheek pressed onto the cool wood. Through sandy-brown strands of hair I watched everyone race from the room. Lexie slowed at the doorway. She waved her homemade Harry Potter wand at me and gave me a small smile before Nakessa appeared behind her and tugged on her arm.

"Louisa," Mrs. Snyder said, drawing my attention to her. "Your test."

I glanced at the doorway. My friends had left. Soon they'd be acting out the play and eating English candy. Without me.

Mrs. Snyder tapped my test with a red ballpoint pen. "I've put the correct spelling by each misspelled word to help you out. Write each one three times. Lock it in your brain." She put her fingers to the side of her head. She pretended to turn a key while making a clicking sound. "Then use the word in a sentence."

If only it were that easy. "That's exactly what I did with my mom. All weekend."

"I know it isn't easy for you, Louisa."

Rub it in, why don't you! "It's impossible," I muttered.

"Pardon me?"

"Nothing." I glared at my paper.

"Just take your time. No need to rush—and no replacing the spelling words this time when you write your sentences. Stick to the words on the list. You have a vast spoken vocabulary, Louisa. I'd like to see those big words on the written page."

I peered up through my eyelashes. Shadow Phantom glided across the room and sat at her desk. A cough rumbled in her chest. She glanced at me. "Go on. Get started."

I really had studied all weekend. Every time

Mom tested me, I got four words wrong, which was frustrating enough, but they were never the same four words. I gritted my teeth. It was more than frustrating. It made me so, so...**angry!**

Hot fury bubbled in my chest. It expanded, oozing throughout my entire body. I felt like I might explode. In fact, I wanted to. I pressed down on my pencil. The lead snapped.

"Good," I murmured, as the flames of fury flickered out. I stared at the first word I had missed. I couldn't believe it. **Frustrating**. I had misspelled **frustrating**. That was literally ironic.

I grabbed two new pencils from my desk, just in case I rage-broke another. I printed each letter in the word **frustrating**, then checked and double checked that I'd put them in the right order.

Being hopeless at spelling words is totally frustrating because I am really good at knowing what they mean. Mom says ever since I could talk, I've been a collector of words. She says I'm a wordsmith. I can talk the talk, but no way can I spell the spell.

The point is, the most frustrating thing about **frustrating** is that I know the dictionary definition by heart: causing annoyance or upset because of an inability to change or achieve something.

And I really, really know about being unable to achieve something. Like a lot.

# Chapter 4

# Five-dollar Words

**W**hen I had to write out sentences on my test, I ditched the word **frustrating**, which is a five-dollar word. That's what Mom calls big words. She says they're worth more in a sentence. She says a lot of weird stuff like that. On my test, I had replaced those ginormous words and filled the paper with ten-cent words. Grade two words. Words I could **mostly** spell.

I glanced at what I had written.

Speling is buging ME.

I had drawn myself being attacked by the

alphabet. Letter **s** had wrapped itself around my legs. **O** circled my head and covered my eyes, while **u** and **v** clamped onto my hands. Cartoon me was a pretty close likeness to real me. Drawing. Another thing I'm good at that Shadow Phantom doesn't appreciate.

Mrs. Snyder had written in large red letters, **Not funny.** Oh. And she had corrected my spelling with that same annoying red pen.

Who wouldn't want to scream? Giving up, however, is much easier. My inner scream melted, like ice cream on a scorching July day. July. My favorite month when I can spend every single day outside....

My gaze drifted to the window. It skipped over the kids playing on the tarmac, to the play structure behind, finally resting on our tall oak tree. My friends were sitting beneath its branches. Lexie gathered up a heaping armful of fall leaves and threw them in the air over Nakessa's head. An ache deep in my chest thrummed to life. They were having **sooooo** much fun. If only I—

"Louisa!" The Shadow Phantom snapped. "Stay on task."

Caught daydreaming. For the million-zillionth time. My eyes returned to my test. Maybe I shouldn't have doodled my name all over the paper. A thirty-six-letter name sure didn't leave much room for corrections. Mom should have named me something simple, like Lou Fox, which is my dream name. I'm ditching my thirty-six letters for those easy six letters as soon as I turn eighteen.

Until then, I'm stuck with being named after my great-grandma, Louisa, who Mom thinks I look like. This is **pre-pos-ter-ous**, a five-dollar word meaning absolutely absurd. In this case it's also laughable, since the only picture we have of her is an old black-and-white photo of the back of her head. Apparently, Mom can sense our spiritual connection.

Weird. My mother has alternative views about everything. But she might be right about me and Great-grandma Louisa. Apparently, ancient Louisa had as much use for school as me, but back in her day it was okay to quit in sixth grade. Which means, if I'd lived in the olden times, I'd only have had to slog through one more year of torture. Then I would have been free to do whatever I wanted: write plays imagining brand-new worlds, or join a traveling Cirque du Soleil troupe—my backup plan in case my plays flop on Broadway. Cirque du Soleil is always looking for extra-bendy people like me. I made this observation to my parents over the summer holidays. They both laughed, and Dad tousled my hair, calling me his number one comedian.

Apparently, it's illegal these days to be an elementary school dropout. In the meantime, I'll just have to keep working on my plays and cartwheels...and putting up with Mrs. Snyder.

# Chapter 5

# Mistakes. So Many Mistakes.

Laughter echoed from the hallway and tore me from my work. Okay, that is a huge exaggeration. A tiny ant whispering "Hey, Lou. Drop your pencil!" could have torn my attention away from spelling.

Oh. Speaking of baby ants, maybe we could work those into our play!

Within seconds of the baby-ant distraction the recess bell rang, and Lexie and Nakessa sped into the classroom seconds ahead of the others.

"Lou!" Lexie called, as she raced around the desks. "We missed you!"

*"Lou, Lou, we missed you,"* sang Nakessa. *"There's no one in the world like...youuuu!"* If it was up to her, all our plays would be musicals. Even our current ghost story.

Whoever heard of singing ghosts? Although singing ants might work. "Aw, you guys." I laughed. Then I remembered the English candy. My laughter stopped. "Did you eat all the candy?"

Lexie plunked a smallish, pink-and-white striped paper bag on her desk. "No way. We didn't have one single piece. Candy can wait until lunch."

All my jealousy slipped away. I might be academically challenged, but when it came to friends, I was gifted.

"There's no way Mrs. Snyder will keep you over lunch too," Nakessa whispered. "She's not actually mean. She just wants you to do well."

I wish I had Nakessa's positive attitude about our teacher, but I wasn't one of Grammers' hound dogs wishing to be an eagle. "I dunno," I said. "I'm pretty sure Mrs. Snyder hates me to my bones."

"Aw, she doesn't hate you, Lou-ba-doo." Lexie sank into her chair. "Nobody could hate you."

Nakessa grabbed my pencils and began to rap a funky rhythm on my desk.

"All right, class. Take your seats," called

Mrs. Snyder. She glared at me, her eyeballs burning a hole in my forehead. "Louisa, are you distracting your friends?"

"Wh-who? Me?" I looked up at Nakessa.

Nakessa's cheeks flushed pink. She waved the pencils in the air. "It was m—"

"I'm sure you don't want to spend lunch with me, do you Louisa?" Mrs. Snyder said, as if Nakessa had turned invisible.

No way was I going to miss lunch with my friends. I stood up. "I didn't do any—"

"Lou," Lexie whispered, cutting me off. "Don't argue. You'll make it worse." She tugged on her ear. She only did that when she was nervous or worried.

I plunked onto my chair.

"Well, Louisa?" Mrs. Snyder coughed into a tissue. "Are we spending lunchtime together?"

"No, Mrs. Snyder." My voice trembled. Not only did I not want to spend lunch with her, I wished I never, **ever** had to spend another second with her. I wished she would just disappear. *Poof!* Like one of my daydreams that she kept ruining.

"I didn't think so. It's too nice a day to be inside," Mrs. Snyder said with a self-satisfied smirk. "Now class, let's move on to math."

Math. I groaned. Great. This was the worst day ever.

"Missing lunch." I muttered so quietly even teensy singing ants wouldn't have heard me. Wasn't that some sort of human rights violation? I mean, how could anyone go all day without eating? Thinking about missing a meal made my stomach growl in protest.

I sighed and stared out the window again, which I now know I should not have done. That was my second mistake of the day. Charcoal-gray clouds had begun to glide across the sky. A gust of wind whipped the branches of our oak tree, scattering leaves. Another gust, far stronger, rattled the window. Huh. The sunny fall day had vanished. "A storm's coming!" Uh-oh. I turned to Lexie. "Did I just say that out loud?" I whispered.

"Very loud," she whispered back.

"Louisa!" Mrs. Snyder snapped. "I think it's time you took a walk to the principal's office. I'll buzz down."

My eyes jerked to the front of the room. Mrs. Snyder shook her head at me, frowning her face into a spider web of wrinkles. She had warped herself into a human storm in no time flat. As she moved toward the intercom, the unfairness of being sent to the office, swept over me. "A storm **is** coming."

I shouldn't have uttered one word. Lexie had already warned me not to argue with Mrs. Snyder.

That was my third mistake of the day.

Mrs. Snyder put her hands on her hips. "Louisa—"

"You'll be thanking me if my warning saves you all from being ripped apart in a tornado." Go big or go home. That's what Grammers always says. I chose big.

Bad choice. And my fourth mistake of the day.

"Do those look like tornado clouds to you?" she shouted.

Whispers filled the room.

"Maybe," I said. Which wasn't a total lie, since I had no clue what tornado clouds looked like.

"Louisa!" Mrs. Snyder's voice rose even higher. "Those are **not** tornado clouds." She coughed, grabbed her water bottle from her desk, and took a long sip. "Children, they are just—" Her voice cracked. She took another sip. "—regular rain clouds."

"Are you sure?" Big Jack asked, standing. He glanced over to the door. "A twister ripped the roof off my cousin's barn last summer."

Mrs. Snyder cleared her throat. "Jack, we're not on a farm in the open prairie. Very few tornados have hit Winnipeg."

"Very few?" Sophia Wabash cupped her hands above her eyes and pressed her face against the glass.

"Does that mean some have?" asked Little Jack.

"How many are very few, do you think?" Big Jack's face paled. "Five or six...or more?"

"Class. That's enough," Mrs. Snyder said, her voice now very calm and very low—all serious-teacher-business sounding. "Louisa. To. The. Office."

I got up from my chair and slunk to the door.

"*Ooooh*. She's in trouble," somebody whispered.

A few kids started laughing. Quickly the giggles turned to a chorus that filled the classroom. They were laughing at **me**. Heat rushed up my neck. When my hand touched the cool metal doorknob it was like a match igniting. The embers of fury that had raged against my spelling test flared.

"That's quite enough class," Mrs. Snyder said. "Now off you go, Louisa. To the office. Principal Muswagam will be waiting for you."

"*Ooooh*. The principal," someone taunted.

This time I was pretty sure the voice belonged to Big Jack, but I couldn't think straight, because that fury in my chest exploded in a huge ball of flames. That's the exact moment I made the fifth and worst mistake of the day. I spun to face Mrs. Snyder.

"I hate you!" My throat tightened. Tears gushed from my eyes like water from a faucet.

"I wish—I wish you were dead!"

Mrs. Snyder's eyes widened. A cough, long and dry, erupted from her chest.

A sob tumbled from my mouth. I swallowed the next one as I yanked the door open.

"Louisa!" Mrs. Snyder cried out after me.

I tore down the hallway and raced past the library, skidding around the corner. Beyond the school office. Out the front door.

# Chapter 6

# U-nique

As I raced down the steps a gust of wind whipped my hair across my face. I swiped it away with my arm and stumbled to a stop. Tears cooled on my cheeks. I didn't know where to go. If I went around the building to the playground, everyone would see me. No way.

I needed a moment to clear my head—to calm down. I considered the clump of nearly bare trees that surrounded the teachers' picnic tables. That would have to do. I dried my face with my shirtsleeve as I stomped across the grass. I slid to the ground, resting my back against the largest of the three trees. It wasn't big like our oak tree out back, but it would do. Mean Mrs. Snyder would never let me go out for recess again. Not after—

I cringed. I'd told her I wished she were dead! I was in big, big trouble. Again. I hugged my legs tight to my chest, rested my head on my knees, and closed my eyes. If only Mrs. Snyder wasn't so horrible. Who wouldn't blow their top if they were tormented by a teacher? If only she'd listened to me...or Nakessa!

"Louisa?"

I knew that voice well. Principal Muswagam. We'd spent a lot of time together this year. A teensy, tiny groan passed my lips. What can I say? I'm a professional groaner. "Yes, it's me," I replied, keeping my eyes closed. "The one and only." If only I had Lexie's homemade wand, I could magically zap myself into another universe.

"May I sit with you?" Mrs. Muswagam asked.

I shrugged. "It is the teachers' area. I guess I should ask you if I can sit here."

Mrs. Muswagam laughed. "That's true. You have a very unique way of seeing the world."

I peeked at the principal from the corner of my eye. She sat cross-legged close to me. Pretty impressive for an oldish lady. She's plumper and

older than Mom, but not nearly as old and plump
as Grammers. Mrs. Muswagam's dark brown hair
had only a few gray streaks in it. Grammers' was
one hundred percent gray. "You are a very unique
principal."

Mrs. Muswagam tilted her head to the side,
a small smile on her face. "I'll take that as a
compliment." She piled leaves onto her knee. "Did
you mean it as a compliment?"

"Yeah," I lifted my head to look fully at Mrs.
Muswagam. "I guess I did."

"'Unique' is a pretty interesting word. You know
what it means, right?"

"Yup. One of a kind."

"Exactly." Mrs. Muswagam picked up a red
maple leaf that was larger than her hand. She
smiled. "Being unique can be frustrating. Sometimes
it can be very, very frustrating." She handed me
the leaf. "Sometimes it can even be lonely."

I squinted at her, sandwiching the cool maple
leaf between my hands. How did she know how
I felt? "Are you a mind reader?"

Mrs. Muswagam's smile broadened, and her
eyes twinkled. "No, and I'm glad I'm not. Can
you imagine knowing everyone's thoughts?" She
laughed. "I'd never sleep again!"

My grin grew as she kept laughing.

Then, my principal snort-laughed! A

snort-laugher! I couldn't believe it. She was definitely the most unique principal I'd ever met.

"It looks like it might rain. How about we go inside and talk?" she suggested.

"Okay." I knew I didn't have a choice, but it was nice she asked.

I followed Mrs. Muswagam back into the school, past the secretary, and right into her office.

"Take a seat," Mrs. Muswagam pointed to the chairs that sat around a small round table.

I slid into the closest swivel chair and spun in a circle. Mrs. Muswagam had made a lot of changes to the office since becoming our principal last year. My favorite one was the spinning chairs.

A large dream catcher hung in the window that looked onto the schoolyard. Gray goose feathers dangled from the ends of leather laces threaded with brightly colored beads. Her kokum had made it for her. **Kokum** is Cree for **grandmother**. Mrs. Muswagam told me all about her kokum the first time I was sent to her office. Our grandmothers sounded a lot alike.

"How's your latest play coming along?" Mrs. Muswagam asked, as she closed the door.

"I'm still working on the details. *The Haunting at Lakeside School* is my first ghost story."

"Sounds intriguing. Mrs. Snyder is very impressed by your imagination. She also said you're a remarkable artist."

I stopped spinning. I'd impressed Mrs. Snyder? "You talked about me? I...wow."

Mrs. Muswagam chuckled. "You don't need to look so surprised. All the teachers come to me about students they're concerned for."

"Oh." Now I was a concern. That sounded way more like Mrs. Snyder.

"Anyway," Mrs. Muswagam said, "I'd love to see your play when you're ready for an audience."

"We just do it for ourselves—Lexie, Nakessa, and I. We've never had a real audience before— besides our parents, and they don't really count."

"All that hard work and no audience?"

I shrugged. "Maybe one day."

"Let's hope one day happens soon." Mrs. Muswagam pulled a game off the shelf and put it on the round table in front of me. "Can you set that up for me?"

"We've never played this one before." I tugged the lid off the box. Inside was a bunch of long black tiles. Each tile had a pattern of different colored shapes on it.

"It's new. You're the first student to play it. It's similar to dominos, but you match shapes or colors instead."

"Huh." It sounded like something Nakessa's little sisters would like.

"Ah, you think it's too simple?" Mrs. Muswagam asked. "There's strategy to master." Mrs. Muswagam opened her top drawer and pulled out two erasers. The kind you shove on the end of your pencil. "If you win, you can choose either this very sad blue hound dog or this even sadder green alien."

"The alien guy is missing his nose."

"Aha! Maybe he never had a nose. He is extraterrestrial after all."

I laughed. A game-playing, funny principal. More than unique. Maybe **she** was an alien. A Shadow Phantom for a teacher. An alien for a principal.
If this was a play, no one would believe it.

"Out on the front lawn," Mrs. Muswagam said, as she placed a tile with an orange triangle down, "that was an unusual place for me to find you."

"Yeah." I placed a blue triangle tile next to it.

I'd been dreading this moment. The Chat.
I knew Mrs. Muswagam would eventually make me talk about what happened. She always does.

"I-I guess I snapped. It's sort of…" I looked at the alien. *If only he would beam me out of here. I bet he might even have an alien ray gun that could zap me down in size so I'd fit into—*

"Louisa."

"Right. Sorry. Drifted."

"Mrs. Snyder sent you to the office for a reason."

"I got really frustrated, and everyone started laughing at me."

"That sounds rough."

"Yeah, it was and…" I glanced up at Mrs. Muswagam. She tilted her head. I dropped my gaze to the game. "I sort of blew up at Mrs. Snyder."

"Oh."

"I didn't mean to. The words just…rushed out of my mouth."

"You must have been very frustrated."

There it was, the word of the day again. My gaze flew from the game to Mrs. Muswagam. She was nearly exactly right. "I was **extremely** frustrated. She kept threatening to make me skip lunch and stay inside with her."

"Skip lunch?"

"Yeah, and it's not right to make a kid miss a meal. In fact, I think it's against the Charter of Rights and Freedoms—"

"Lou." Mrs. Muswagam smiled. "You must have misunderstood Mrs. Snyder. She would never make you miss a meal. She meant you'd miss going outside with your friends **after** you ate."

"Oh." I pressed a tile to the table with one finger and flicked it with my other hand, spinning it in place. "I guess that makes more sense than starving me."

"We don't starve students at Lakewood, and I

had a quick word with your teacher. You won't be inside for lunch break." Mrs. Muswagam placed a blue diamond tile onto the table.

"Really?" That was a huge relief.

"Yes, and I know it's hard, but let's find a way to manage your outbursts. If you recognize the signs before you lose control, you'll be better able to think before you act. Listen to your body—when your heart starts beating fast, or when your face gets super-hot, or—"

"When my hands ball into fists?"

"Exactly. Warning signs. So, what can you do when you realize your emotions are getting the better of you?"

"Bite my tongue?" I stopped spinning the tile.

Mrs. Muswagam smirked. "I was thinking more along the lines of taking some deep breaths, or you could take a walk to cool down. I have faith in you, Louisa."

"You do?"

"Of course! It's not every school that has a soon-to-be-famous playwright in fifth grade."

**Brrrriiinng!**

"I'll tidy up the game. You head back to class." Mrs. Muswagam said. "And remember to take some deep breaths, or—"

"Go for a walk. I'll try to remember." I swiveled in my chair, fighting hard not to roll my eyes.

"Oh, and Louisa," Mrs. Muswagam pointed to the game. "You're way ahead. Pick a prize and then off you go to class. You got this!"

"Well, yee-haw! This lonesome critter needs a home." I stuffed the noseless green alien eraser into my pocket, then leapt to my feet.

"Uhm," I hesitated in her doorway. "Thanks."

"My door is always open."

I didn't rush from the office. I was in no hurry to see Mrs. Snyder after yelling at her. When I snail-strolled around the last corner that led to our classroom, the Bendables ran down the hall to me.

"Are you okay?" Lexie asked, draping her arm around my shoulder.

"Yeah."

"Are you in big trouble?" Nakessa asked. She swooped her braids on top of her head, slipping an elastic from her wrist around them. Like always, her bundle of hair looked like a second head. It stayed upright for exactly three seconds before sliding down to cover an ear.

I giggled.

"Don't say it," Nakessa said, trying to scowl at me. Her lips quivered, fighting a smile. We knew she not-so-secretly loved making us laugh when her floppy bun went rogue.

"It's slip sliding away!" I said.

Nakessa tried to swallow her laugh, but it only

51

got stuck in her throat, until she lost the laugh-battle. **"Haaacck!"**

Lexie might be the most academically gifted, but if Nakessa's laugh played on Broadway, it would win its own Tony Award.

Lexie held out the pink-and-white candy bag from England. "Take one. Enjoy the Nakessa show." Once Nakessa bark-laughed, there was no stopping her.

Nakessa, unable to speak, wrapped her arms around her middle and stomped a foot.

I pulled out a small round candy from the paper bag. "What are they?"

"English bonbons," Lexie answered.

Nakessa's laughter had now entered its final stage. Still holding her stomach, she leaned against the lockers.

I popped the bonbon into my mouth. My eyes widened, as tart lemon tickled my tastebuds. "Chewy."

**"Haaacck!"** Tears streamed down Nakessa's face.

Lexie's eyebrows shot high. "You like?"

"I **love**! English bonbons are my new favorite. Now, about our play..."

# Chapter 7

# Abnormal Normal Sandwich

When the three of us wandered back into the classroom, Nakessa was still catching her breath from laughing so hard. Thankfully, Mrs. Snyder was nowhere in sight. Instead, our lunch monitor, Mr. Diaz, stood at the front of the room holding a clipboard. As usual he wore a sweater-vest. "*Senhoras*, you are six minutes late," he said. Mr. Diaz has been trying to teach our class Portuguese for the past two years. So far, all we've mastered are the days of the week, colors, numbers up to ten, and zoo animals. If anyone wants to know if we have three red hippos, we're good to go.

"*Três hipopótamos vermelhos*," I said.

Mr. Diaz laughed. He finds me a delight. He said so back in fourth grade. Why couldn't he be our teacher? Unfortunately, lunch monitors can't become teachers simply because you want them to. I asked Mrs. Muswagam about it last week. Apparently, you need a lot of training to be a teacher. All I know is, my life would be a lot more enjoyable if I didn't have a Shadow Phantom for a teacher, watching my every move.

"Your pronunciation is, as always, perfect— *perfeita*." He wrote both words on the whiteboard. "As you can see, the Portuguese is very close to English. Simple."

Simple for some. But for me, trying to remember spelling in two languages is not double the work like it would be for anyone else. For me, it's more like ten times harder. What's totally weird though, is I can parrot accents and do impressions really well.

Being parrot-like is not exactly helpful in my day-to-day studies. Mrs. Snyder certainly doesn't appreciate my talents. Last week, I was under our oak tree at recess entertaining half the class with my impression of her during roll call. I had no idea she hovered behind me, until her nasally voice stopped me cold. "If only you could do an impression of seven times eight, Louisa. Now that would be a productive use of your time."

Mr. Diaz would have been impressed. Mrs. Snyder e-mailed my mom.

I grabbed my lunch from my cubby, sniffing it as I plunked onto my seat. Nothing stinky. No fried onion and tofu sandwiches. No pickle and egg salad sandwiches. And, thankfully, none of my least favorite: stone-cold leftover meatloaf. My mother could not be trusted with lunch.

I glanced at Lexie's desk. In a neat row she had lined up five small reusable glass containers, each one filled with delicious food. Slices of marble cheese, seeded crackers, cherry tomatoes, snap peas, and, as always, Jell-O. Today it was grape. Lexie's favorite. And then a small pile of White Rabbit candies. They were the Bendables' number one favorite candy. Lexie's grandma—her *nainai*—slips handfuls in her lunch kit a few times a week. And why are White Rabbits our favorite? Rice paper. It's this melt-on-your-tongue deliciousness that wraps around a chewy, creamy vanilla candy. Oh, and they have the cutest little bunny on the wrapper. I stared at the candies on her desk and wished Grammers lived with us.

"What did your mom pack today?" Lexie asked.

"I'm afraid to look." I sighed. "Why can't my mom be more like yours?"

"Because she's all mine!" Lexie scooped up a spoonful of Jell-O. "Besides, your mom is way more fun. I mean, she's the only mom who camps out with us in the backyard. She's the only reason we get to watch shooting stars every summer. My mother would never do that."

Nakessa sighed. "Neither would mine. She's too terrified of bugs to spend a night outside."

"Here goes..." I unzipped my lunch kit and lifted a small baggie. It held a very normal-looking sandwich. "Ham and cheese...on white bread!"

"Woah. That's weird. I bet there's some sort of strange sauce on it. Remember last week when she slathered your eggplant sandwich with jalapeño jelly?" Nakessa asked.

I remembered. That lunch ranked in the top ten of all-time lunch disasters. Carefully I pulled out the sandwich, peeking under the bread. "White goop."

"It looks like mayo," said Nakessa.

"I didn't even know you owned mayonnaise," Lexie said.

"We don't." This was weird, even for Mom. It might sound like a minor addition to a sandwich, but in the Fitzhenry-O'Shaughnessy household it was huge. Finding white bread **and** mayonnaise in our house was like finding life on Mars. Something was up.

I took a bite. I smiled. White bread and mayo sandwiches were almost too easy to eat. I felt like one of those kids in a Disney sitcom. The TV version of a normal kid. I jumped to my feet. "That's it! Grammers is coming to visit. Last time Mom fed me a normal lunch was when Grammers came to stay two Christmases ago."

"Grandmas are the best," Nakessa said, her voice soft. "When I was little, my Grandma Kaur used to make the best curry. Whenever my parents went to the movies or out to dinner, she'd babysit us. She'd sing us Hindi lullabies when she tucked us in bed. Before she got sick."

Lexie set down her container of grapes. "You must really miss her."

"Yeah. I think of her almost every day."

I couldn't imagine Grammers dying. My mind drifted, thinking of the last time she visited. Mom insisted that everything had to be perfect. Well, perfect according to Grammers and according to Grammers, ham and cheese on white bread is lunchtime perfection. The problem for Mom is that perfection of any kind is not her Modus Operandi. Her MO is, "Relax and don't sweat the small stuff."

When Dad told Mom to relax and not sweat the small stuff in the middle of Grammers Prep, Mom had an atom-bomb explosion. I swear, her hair lifted from her head like a mushroom cloud. Her voice went super quiet. "Not. Funny," she said.

I bit into my ham and mayo sandwich—a tasty clue. When I got home, I hoped the house just might be under Not. Funny. Grammers. Prep.

Or maybe Grammers was already there!

# Chapter 8

# Further Mom
# Weirdness

For the average fifth grader, my house is a five-minute walk from school. For me it takes anywhere from five to twenty-five minutes. If school's been a nonstop train wreck, I usually need some quiet time. On those days I meander home at a snail's pace.

And on those snail-slow days, I normally stop in front of Mr. Popowich's house. He's always moving his garden gnomes around and adding new ones. Anyway, even though I'd had a horrendous day, I didn't even slow when I neared

Mr. Popowich's house. I was home in a record two and a half minutes.

Why? Because I was hoping Grammers had already arrived.

"Mom!" I called as the door slammed shut behind me. I kicked off my sneakers and dumped my backpack on top of them. I tore down the hallway and slid across the kitchen floor like I always do, hoping to find Mom and Grammers at the kitchen table. Empty, except for the pile of cardboard boxes I skidded into. The top box toppled over, thudding to the floor. Books spilled out. I picked one up. *Babies, Toddlers, and Teens.* Mom must be deep into her cleaning if she was clearing out old books.

I dropped it back onto the pile. Where was my grandmother? "Mom!!!" I bellowed.

"Down here." Her faint voice traveled up from the basement.

I darted to the top of the basement staircase and placed a hand on each railing. Kicking my legs out far, I swung down the stairs. My toes touched down on every third or fourth step as I propelled myself along. I counted the seconds, landing at the bottom with my arms out in a perfect gymnast's pose. Three and a smidge seconds. Good thing Mom didn't see me. She always worried I'd break my legs, but I never hurt myself. Well, rarely.

Stacks of carboard boxes covered the rec-room sofa. My old blocks, dolls, and fabric baby books were piled high on the coffee table. "Where are you?" I called.

"The storage room. I'd love a hand."

I zipped into the storage room. Every box and plastic tub had been taken off the shelves and opened. Clothes and lids were strewn everywhere. All thoughts of Grammers drifted from my mind. "Woah. What happened?"

"Just trying to find something." Mom peeked up over a stack of boxes, at the back of the narrow room. As always, her paint smock covered up her clothes.

"Did a bomb literally explode in here?" I squeezed between my old stroller and highchair to move farther into the room.

"No bombs." She smiled, opening another box. She shook her head. "Not here." She turned and pointed to the last box on the top shelf. "Cross your fingers that's the one I need." She looked at me. "Come on. Cross those digits."

I crossed my fingers.

"Only good energy allowed in this room."

Good energy. See? Weird.

Mom stood on a large plastic tub, reaching high.

"You're too short," I said. "Maybe wait for Dad to get—"

Mom jumped and her fingers snagged the edge of the box, moving it just enough that she could drag it down. That's another thing about Mom. If there's something she wants to do, she just goes out and does it. She smiled down at me, wobbling on the tub. "Yup! This is it!"

"What's inside?" I shimmied around the highchair to get closer.

"You'll see." She stepped to the floor, hiding the box behind her. "No peeking....Oh..." Her face suddenly paled. "I need to scoot to the restroom." She climbed over a shorter pile of boxes. "Meet me in the kitchen. I want to hear all about your day."

"It was a doozy." I squished flat to my old crib so Mom and her mystery box could get past.

Why was Mom wasting time messing around? Didn't she want things to be as perfect as last time Grammers visited? I shrugged and bounded from the storage room, past the boxes in the rec room, and up the stairs. Mom still hadn't mentioned my grandmother. How long did she intend to keep the secret? I couldn't wait until she arrived.

I sat at the kitchen table while Mom poured me a glass of almond milk. She stacked three store-bought cookies in front of me. Store. Bought. Cookies. First mayonnaise, then white bread, now store-bought cookies. Utter cookie joy filled me. We have never, ever had anything but homemade.

Mom glanced at the mystery box on the kitchen counter. She'd spread a tea towel over it, so I couldn't see the words written on the cardboard. "I have something to tell you," she said, and clasped her hands. She smiled, her face no longer pale.

"Grammers is coming!" I blurted. I couldn't help myself. I'd been home close to ten minutes already. "I know you love surprises, and this was likely a humongous one, but come on, you know waiting is excruciating for me." **Ex-cru-ci-at-ing**. Beyond painful.

"Yes, but Lou—"

"So, when is she supposed to get here?"

"I'm afraid Grammers isn't the surprise."

"Oh." My heart lurched. Grammers always makes things better, and this school year hadn't been stellar. It had been **a-bys-mal**, meaning extremely bad, horrible, awful, and terrible. The exact opposite of stellar. And Grammers not coming to visit was a terrible, awful five-dollar-word feeling.

Mom slid the towel off the mystery box as she plunked it onto the table. She tapped the top.

I stared at it, feeling abysmal. "Your good news is in an old box?"

"Come look."

I stood. Mom swiveled the box, so the writing faced me. Messy, scrawled handwriting. It might as well have been another language. "Huh?"

"It says 'Pregnancy.'" She pointed at two more neatly printed, big black words.

I read them slowly. "Fav...or...ite Outfits." I looked at Mom. "Okay."

"I wore these when I was pregnant with you, and I had a perfect pregnancy. And a perfect baby." Mom tore the box open and pulled out a bunch of giant shirts. "They brought me good luck."

I was far from perfect, but okay. She looked like she wanted me to say something. "Uhm, yay! Good luck's...good!"

She shook her head, laughing. Her weirdness was increasing by the second. "Lou," she said. "You're finally going to be a big sister."

"Really?" A big sister. I never thought that would happen. Excitement raced through me. My legs jiggled like Lexie's grape Jell-O. "I'm really and truly going to be a big sister?" I've wanted that all my life. "You're pulling some sort of prank on me, right?"

"No pranks." Her eyes got all watery. She sat next to me and held my hand.

"But you said you couldn't have any more kids."

"I didn't think I could. I thought you were our one and only miracle."

64

Finally, I was going to be a big sister!

"Now we'll be a two-miracle family. What do you think?" She squeezed my hand.

A smile swallowed my face. "Are we going to find out if it's a boy or a girl? When's it going to be born?" I glanced at Mom's stomach. "That's why your tummy's been getting bigger!"

"Yes." Mom laughed. "But I thought I'd done a good job hiding it."

"Can I name it? What about—wait! Does Dad know?"

"Oh, Louisa Elizabeth." She laughed, pulling me in for a hug. "How I love you."

# Chapter 9

# The Four
# Musketeers

I stared at my computer screen. Lexie and
Nakessa stared back at me from their own
bedrooms. We'd been video chatting for the past
hour to work on the play. I had been tempted to
tell them about becoming a big sister, but I wanted
to tell them in person.

"I think I've got it all down," I said. "Tomorrow
you can look it over and see if I missed anything."

"Okay." Lexie moved closer to her computer's
camera with her arms outstretched. "Sending
virtual hugs. See you at our tree."

"*Tomorrow, tomorrow, there's always tomorrow...*" sang Nakessa as she blew us kisses.

"Later, gators," I said as their faces blinked off the screen.

I clicked on *The Haunting at Lakeside School* document. The large Helvetica font made it way easier for me to read. Last year, my dyslexia tutor suggested I use a software program to help me type out my plays. It's so simple. I talk into the microphone on my laptop, and the program types my words. It works really well, most of the time. One time I said, "She raced down the stairs." The program typed it out as, "Sweet-faced, proud neck bears." What the heck is a proud neck bear? It still makes me laugh. It may not be perfect, but I'd like to personally thank the genius who invented the software. Now, spelling and printing don't hold me back—at least not with my plays.

My bedroom door creaked open. Dad stepped inside, sliding his glasses off. He pinched the bridge of his nose near his eyes, which he always does when he's tired. "Time for bed, Bugaboo."

That's Dad's nickname for me. He likes to change things up—Bug, Buggie, Bug-eyes—so my list of nicknames keeps growing.

"I just have to print this next section for tomorrow. We wrote a whole new scene tonight."

The printer churned as I turned off the computer.

"Awesome." Dad picked up a pair of dirty socks and tossed them, basketball-style, into the laundry basket in the corner. "Swish! Just like the glory days." Even though Dad's not very tall, he became the star player on his high-school team. He reminds us whenever possible. "Any proud neck bears in this play?"

I laughed. "Never."

"Can you believe Mom went to sleep before you again?" Dad asked.

"Yeah, she's been doing that a lot lately." I yawned and climbed into bed.

"Growing a baby is tiring business." He pulled my comforter up to my chin, then folded the edge over so the cool slippery side wouldn't touch my face.

"Guess we won't be The Three Musketeers anymore," I said.

"Nope, in a few months we'll be even better— The Four Musketeers!"

"Is that even a thing?" My pillow puffed around my head like a giant marshmallow.

"Actually, it is. The baby can be d'Artagnan. In *The Three Musketeers* novel, d'Artagnan arrives later in the story. Just like our baby's arriving later in our family. Huh. D'Artagnan Fitzhenry-O'Shaughnessy. It has kind of a nice—"

"No! Dad, please no. I don't want my little brother to be teased his entire life."

"D'Artagnan could be a girl."

"Absolutely not."

Dad chuckled. "Kidding. Pretty sure Mom wouldn't be too happy with it either." He tucked my stuffed purple pig, Pearl, under the covers next to me. Pearl's squashed snout brushed my cheek. She was my very first stuffed animal. Grammers gave her to me at the hospital just hours after I was born.

"You never got to tell us about your day," said Dad. "Sorry about that."

"It's okay. Talking about the baby is more fun than talking about my crummy day."

"More run-ins with Mrs. Snyder?"

"Yup. She's some sort of Shadow Phantom. She hears everything. She sees everything. She's everywhere all at once!"

Dad smiled. "That would be unsettling. Tell me what happened."

My stomach twisted with anger. "She's totally out to get me."

Dad looked over his glasses at me. "Really? A teacher, whose profession is to help kids, is out to get the most adorable ten-year-old in her class? No!" Dad raised his hand, as if to stop me from interrupting and shook his head dramatically.

Hair, the exact shade of mine, flopped across his forehead.

I tried hard not to smile.

"No, no, no! I should've said, the most adorable ten-year-old she has ever taught in her very, very long career."

My anger flickered and died. "Dad, stop it." I laughed. "I'm serious."

"Sorry. Yes. Carry on." He looked at my stuffie. "And that's enough out of you, Pearl."

"Dad!"

"Right. Listening."

"Okay. First Mrs. Snyder picked on me about my spelling, then she picked on me about daydreaming, then she made me stay in at recess."

"That sounds pretty rough."

"It was. She's always after me. It isn't fair. She never picks on anyone else."

"Never is a very long time."

"Okay, she hardly ever picks on anyone else." I clenched my covers. "You're supposed to be on my side."

"I am, but Louisa, **were** you daydreaming?" Dad slid his glasses off and cleaned them on his T-shirt.

I shrugged. "A little bit, maybe."

He put his glasses back on and waggled his

bushy eyebrows at me. "Anything else you want to share?"

"Uhm…" I looked away. Did I have to tell him about screaming at Mrs. Snyder? Couldn't I just pretend it didn't happen? And that's when I lied to Dad for the first time ever. "There's nothing else to share."

Dad tilted his head. His brown eyes looked right into mine. "Alrighty, if you say so."

"I do."

He kissed my forehead, just like always. And his stubbly whiskers tickled my face. As usual.

"Just remember, Bugaboo. You can tell me anything."

"I know."

"Goodnight, sleep tight, don't let the bed bugs bite," Dad said, as he does every night. It's our Dad/Daughter MO.

And just like I always do, I replied, "But they can't get me, and they can't get you, because I'm the Mighty Bugaboo!"

Dad flicked off my light.

"Oh, Dad!" I bolted upright. "I forgot to ask Mom to find some old sheets. I need them tomorrow for ghost costumes in our play."

"Leave it with me. I'll take care of it." He left the room and closed my door.

Within a few seconds, the solar system

glow-in-the-dark stickers brightened on my ceiling.
Dad had stuck them there after we went to the
planetarium when I was seven. For a full year all
my plays had been set on different planets; Mars,
Jupiter, Pluto, and of course I invented a new
planet: Louturn.

I lay still. After a few seconds, I whispered to
the tiny universe what I should have admitted
to Dad. "I told my teacher I wished she was
dead." I knew I'd been cruel, but she hated me.
I'd only been getting back at her. The problem
was, being mean didn't feel very good. My eyes
burned. Tears trickled out the corners of my eyes
toward my ears. Swiping them away, I rolled onto
my side. I'd have to try harder to stay calm. I'd
have to be better. I needed to stop getting into
trouble.

# Chapter 10

# Lies
# and More Lies

Dad slipped on his shoes as I swung my backpack over my shoulder. Yawning, I sat at the bottom of the staircase that led to the second floor.

"No, Paul. Not that bow tie," Mom said.

"Nadine! How dare you?" Dad's eyes went wide, one hand on his chest, as he pretended to be offended. "It's my favorite."

Mom laughed. "SpongeBob clothing is no grown adult's favorite anything."

Dad looked at his watch. "I don't have time to find another."

"That's fine. Sometimes, like in art, less is more." Mom kissed him on the cheek, then slid off the bow tie.

"Let's go." Dad pulled me up.

I slouched under the weight of my backpack. "Why couldn't school start at noon?"

"That would suit me just fine." Mom passed me my lunch. "White bread again." Mom had explained over breakfast that pregnant women often crave certain foods. So far for Mom her cravings were mayonnaise, white bread, and store-bought cookies.

I laughed. "Maybe you could start craving fast food."

Mom grimaced. All color rushed from her face. "Oh, no." She covered her mouth with one hand and pushed Dad out of the way with the other. Down the hallway, the bathroom door slammed behind her.

"I don't think we're having burgers anytime soon," Dad said.

"I didn't mean to make her sick."

"As I said last night, growing a baby is hard work." Dad grabbed a cloth bag from the staircase banister. "Don't forget the sheets. Turn."

I spun around. Dad stuffed the bag into my backpack and zipped it up. "Turn back."

As I spun to face Dad, I shot my arms out to

my sides, pretending to lose my balance. "I'm
going to be puking next."

"Funny and gross. You **are** the perfect
daughter." Dad kissed me on the forehead.
"Now get to school." He opened the door for
me. "And no dawdling."

"See ya, Dad." No way would I be late today.
No way would I even take a second look at
Mr. Popowich's gnomes. I had way too much to tell
Lexie and Nakessa.

* * *

As soon as I spotted my friends under our oak
tree, I picked up speed. My backpack thumped
against me as I raced across the grass. Cool
wind blew my hair off my face, and puffy
clouds cast long shadows across the field.

"Lou!" Lexie ran up and gave me a big hug.

We linked arms as we walked to Nakessa,
who hung upside down from the lowest
tree branch. Her braids nearly touched the
ground. Her cheeks were bright red.

"I have the biggest news." I said, dropping my
bag on the ground. "I'll tell you while I stretch."

With my back against the oak tree, I kicked
my right leg high.

Lexie grabbed it and pushed up. "You're not

grounded again, are you?"

"No, why would I be?"

"Because of yesterday—with Mrs. Snyder." She shoved my leg higher.

The back of my thigh burned. "Uhm-no, it wasn't a big deal."

Lexie took one hand away from my leg to tug on her ear. "Really?"

"Yeah," I exhaled. Flexibility's no joke. "My parents were...fine about it." Which wasn't technically a lie. Technically.

"Huh. Your parents aren't usually so fine about you getting into trouble at school." She frowned, returning both hands to my leg stretch.

"They were...this time."

Lexie applied more pressure. I winced.

"My parents would've killed me dead," Nakessa said, still hanging upside down from the tree. She rocked back and forth, reached up, grasped the branch, and pulled her legs free, dropping to the ground.

"Well, my parents...are nice." I pushed against Lexie's hands. "I gotta...stop."

She dropped my leg, and my foot smacked the ground.

"Hey." Nakessa's face reddened. "My parents are nice, too!"

"That's not what I meant. I meant...they're on

my side." I stumbled over my lie. My second in two days. I'd never lied to the Bendables before. My hands began to sweat. "They totally think Mrs. Snyder is mean. In fact, they're going to e-mail her."

"Wow," Lexie said.

The longer I kept talking, the bigger the lie grew. Like Grammers says, "Go big or go home." I went **e-nor-mous**—bigger than big. "Yup and my dad's going to talk to the principal."

Nakessa stepped back, shaking her head. "Wowzers. Remind me not to mess with *Lou, Lou-ba-doo, Lou-ba-doo, ba-doo ba-doo!*" Then she stretched her arms out to the sides and bowed.

I forced a smile to my face. My lips quivered as I wiped my sweaty hands on my jeans.

"Didn't you have some big news?" Lexie asked, popping a candy in her mouth.

"Yeah, I do!" Relieved she'd changed the subject, I pushed the lie away. "I'm going to have a little baby brother or sister."

Nakessa threw her arms in the air. "Wooohooo! You're going to love being a big sister." Nakessa had two little sisters and an older brother.

"Group hug!" Lexie said. "You're going to be the world's best big sister."

"Except for me," said Nakessa.

Lexie laughed. "And me, of course."

We wrapped our arms around each other just as the bell rang.

"All for one and one for all!" Lexie said.

"Ready," I said.

"Steady," Lexie said.

"*Freddy*," Nakessa sang.

"Go Bendables!" We cheered.

What I wasn't ready for was seeing the Shadow Phantom again.

# Chapter 11

# Less of Me

I scurried into the classroom, zipping straight to my cubby to dump off my backpack. Keeping my sights locked on my desk on the far side of the room, I avoided making eye contact with Mrs. Snyder. I slid into my seat, my plan firmly in mind. I would **not** get into trouble. Somehow, I would stay on task. I would not daydream. I would listen to every word Mrs. Snyder uttered. Every. Single. Word. And boy did she like to talk. A chatty Shadow Phantom. Just my luck.

"Today, we will be exploring the three states of

matter," Mrs. Snyder began. "Solids, liquids, and gasses."

"Gasses? Like farting?" Big Jack said, as he took his seat.

Giggles filled the room.

"Settle down, class." Mrs. Snyder shuffled through a stack of papers on her desk.

"Hey, Louisa," Big Jack whispered. He stuck his hand under his red lumberjack shirt. Then he flapped his arm up and down. Fart sounds squawked across the room.

"Ew." I rolled my eyes.

Mrs. Snyder's head popped up. "Who did that?"

Everyone stared at Big Jack. Big Jack smirked. His blue eyes flashed. "It was Sophia Wabash."

Sophia Wabash turned in her chair. She glared at Big Jack. "No, it wasn't! It was you!"

"Jack! That's enough." Mrs. Snyder's voice sounded raspy. "No more lying. Keep up that lying, and no one will trust anything you have to say. And cap off inside."

Red splotches dotted Big Jack's face as he slid off his Jets hockey cap.

Lies. I shrunk down in my desk. First, I lied to Dad. Then to the Bendables. It felt like Mrs. Snyder was talking to me too. But that was impossible. She was a Shadow Phantom, not a mind reader.

# The U-nique Lou Fox

I glanced at Lexie. She already had a pencil, eraser, and science notebook neatly laid out on her desk. Mom's words from the morning flashed in my brain. *Less is more.* I needed to be way less me and far more Lexie.

*That's it!*

I sat up straight. That's how I could get through the day without getting into trouble. I just needed to keep thinking, *What would Lexie do?* and then do it! Seemed simple enough.

Reaching inside my desk, my fingers wrapped around a bunch of pencils. One even had a slightly sharpened end. I searched again and grabbed the noseless green alien eraser and three notebooks. Picking the science notebook, I stuffed the other two back into my desk. The science notebook's cover had caught in my backpack zipper last week, so it was a little torn at the top corner. I smoothed it down. It sprang back up. I pounded it with my fist. Slowly, it bent up again. "It'll have to do," I muttered, setting it next to the pencil and eraser.

I compared my supplies to Lexie's. Technically, they were the same, but Lexie's looked nearly brand new. Mine looked like they had done battle inside my desk. The alien's facial issues didn't help.

"Now, let's begin," Mrs. Snyder said. She coughed again.

I jumped in my seat. Focus. I needed to focus. I gripped the edges of my desk with my hands and stared at my teacher. She gulped a long sip of water. *Stay on task. Focus. Listen. Think like Lexie.* How hard could that be?

It took every single ounce of concentration to stay focused on Mrs. Snyder, while at the same time, trying to be more Lexie. I made it through the first half of the morning without the Shadow Phantom snapping at me, but when the recess bell rang, I needed a nap. I slumped across my desk.

"Come on," Lexie grabbed my hand.

"We need to practice the play," added Nakessa.

**The play!** Those words blasted energy straight to my brain. Jumping from my seat, I darted between the desks and around other students to my cubby. From my backpack I grabbed my bag of ghost bedsheets and the thin binder that held the latest scene for the play. "Let's go!" I called across the sea of chatting heads that bobbed between me and my pals. "Why's everyone moving like snails in peanut butter? Come on, move it! We'll miss recess."

Being the tallest in the class, Sophia Wabash didn't need to stand on her tiptoes to peer over everyone's heads to the doorway. "It's Big Jack," she said. "He's blocking everyone on purpose."

"What? Why?"

She shrugged, yanking on her purple fleece jacket. "I dunno."

"Y'all are slow as molasses." I squeezed through the other students to reach him.

"Oh, hi Louisa." Big Jack blushed and adjusted his baseball cap.

"What seems to be the hold up, son?"

"Huh?" He frowned.

Apparently, Grammers' Southern accent confused him. I switched back to everyday Lou. "What are you doing?"

"As class president, I'm petitioning for a longer recess—"

"Back up that bus, son." Firmly channeling Grammers again, I pointed my finger at his chest. "No way, no how are you the class president."

"Yes I am. Mrs. Snyder said so."

"When?"

Big Jack's face turned crimson, which is a poetic way of saying dark red. "Uhm-ah-yesterday..."

"Liar."

"No, I'm—"

I held my hand up, in the internationally accepted Stop Right There sign. I had no time for this. I had a play to practice. "Just do the petition in the hall. Some of us would like to actually get outside before recess is over."

Big Jack shrugged. "Fine." He muttered and stepped through the doorway.

"And you're not the class president," I said as I stepped past him into the hall. I zipped past the sixth graders' lockers to wait by the water fountain. Like an unclogged drain, the line of kids poured from the classroom. Still no Bendables. "Come on. Come on. Come on." I tapped my binder with my fingers.

Finally, Nakessa and Lexie appeared. "Wow!" Nakessa said when they reached me. "How in the world did you just go from near zombie to the Road Runner in one second?"

"I dunno, but hurry up!" I waved the bag at her. "Don't you want to see the ghost costumes?"

"Singing ghosts?" Nakessa asked.

I laughed. "Maybe!"

The moment we got to our oak tree, Nakessa grabbed my arm. "Oh my gosh, Lou. Big Jack totally likes you."

"What? No, he doesn't." Big Jack, the farting machine?

"Yes, he does. He like-likes you."

"Gross."

"It's true," Lexie said. "Didn't you hear him?"

"Making farting sounds?" I scoffed. "It was impossible not to."

"No, before that. He called your name to get your attention," Lexie said.

"Ick." I held my hand up to stop her. "Don't say another word. It will totally ruin the big reveal of the costumes."

Nakessa yanked the bag from my hand. "Let's see!" She pulled out a sheet, then burst out laughing.

I grabbed it from her, dropping my binder as I did. "Those are my old Fairy Princess sheets! I wanted white ones. Dad totally pranked me. This is his idea of hilarious."

Nakessa held up another set. "Robin Hood!"

Lexie giggled. "Remember when you wrote that play, *Lexie Chan and Her Band of Merry Women*? That was my favorite."

Nakessa draped the Robin Hood sheets over her head. "That's because you were the lead." She slowly raised her arms in front of her, tenting the sheet, and began to sing. "*When there's something strange at Lakeside School. Who you gonna call?*"

"Robin Hood!" Nakessa and Lexie shouted together.

I plunked onto the grass, pulling the binder onto my lap. "Sorry about this."

"Don't worry about it." Lexie sat next to me. "We can still practice our lines."

"Yeah, but I'm the director. Making sure the actors take their parts seriously is the most important part of the job. Otherwise, the play won't turn out right."

Nakessa flipped the sheet back from her face. "Lou, don't get so upset." She sat on the other side of me. "It's not like anyone but us will ever see the play."

"Yeah, that's true." I opened the rings of my binder to remove the new pages I'd written last night. "I have some new lines for you."

Nakessa jumped up. The sheet caught in the wind and ballooned behind her like a parachute. "I will get you," she read, "and every brat in Lakeside School!" She lunged at Lexie.

Lexie rolled across the grass, out of her way. **"Aaaahhhh!"** She scrambled to her feet and

Nakessa chased her around the tree.

"Why do you hate kids so much?" Lexie sounded perfectly terrified.

*Yes!* Hearing my words acted out felt better than landing a front flip. A gentle warmth flowed through my body. I couldn't stop smiling.

Nakessa wildly waved her arms in the air. Her eyes squinting, she grimaced. "Children are a big nuisance. They don't listen. They don't follow directions. And they don't do their..." She looked at me. "...homework?"

"Yeah, I thought the ghost could be the dead principal who's haunting the school."

"Cool." Nakessa nodded her head.

"Did she die at the school?" Lexie asked. "That would be a good reason for her to be stuck at Lakeside."

"Yeah!" The sheet flopped forward, hiding Nakessa's face. She yanked it off, throwing it to the ground. "Her body is gone, but her tormented soul is trapped within—"

"I haven't figured that part out yet," I cut her off. I was the real playwright, not Nakessa.

Nakessa's smile slid from her face. "I was just suggesting—"

"Yeah, I know. Just leave it to me." I knew we were writing the play together, but being an **actual** playwright was my one big, audacious dream. It's the only thing I was really good at. That, and being bendy. And art. Okay, so one of three things. But it was my number one dream.

"Hey, I think we have an audience." Lexie pointed over to the metal bench that sat in front of the play structure. Sophia Wabash, Little Jack, and some other kids were watching us. They clapped. An audience! The three of us bowed. I did a back flip. My heart zinged. All defensive thoughts were squashed by a burning question. Were we ready for the big time?

# Chapter 12

# If Only Every Class Was Art

Back at my desk, I glued my eyes on Mrs. Snyder, determined to stay focused. With the occasional glance at Lexie, I figured it would be a cinch to imitate her every move. Sticking to my plan was the only way to keep Shadow Phantom Snyder off my back.

"Class," Mrs. Snyder said. "Take out your social studies textbook and turn to page thirty-four. Please read the first two paragraphs silently. Then we'll break into our groups to work on the Regional Geography Project for the balance of the afternoon."

Silent reading. Not my favorite. I flipped open the textbook to the right page. The entire page was solid text. Not one chart or illustration. So many words. I groaned.

"You okay?" Lexie whispered.

"Uhm-yeah." I gave her a thumbs-up then drawled like Grammers. "Readin's like lassoin' a bucking bronco with a shoelace. All sorts of tricky, Ma'am."

She giggled.

"Hush. I shouldn't hear voices," Mrs. Snyder said.

*Be more like Lexie*, I reminded myself. Lexie Chan definitely did not groan when reading, or talk when she shouldn't. I grabbed the bookmark that I keep in my desk and placed it under the first sentence. When I block the next line from sight, I can't see those words and mix the two sentences together.

Something fluttered out of the corner of my eye. Something outside. Was it a bird on the window ledge, or a dog in the field? I clenched my teeth. *Do not look. Stay on task.* I slowly read.

*Our coun-try can be...*

I frowned. The next word was a stumper.

*di-divid-ed. Divided!*

I kept going.

*into*

Uh-oh.

*lan-landfo- landform reg-i-ons.*

Huh. That didn't sound right. I decided to ignore the last word and glanced at Lexie. She was deep in thought. Probably thinking landform whatsits were super fascinating. No groaning emerged from Miss Chan. I peeked behind me at Nakessa. She looked as fascinated by the textbook as Lexie. I sighed. Sighing might have to replace groaning if I was going to master being more Lexie and less Lou. Returning to my textbook, I tackled the next sentence. It wasn't much easier. Neither were the next three. Pretty soon my underarms began to sweat. Ick.

Mrs. Snyder coughed. My focus shifted in a nano-second to her. She'd become awfully pale. She actually looked kind of sick. "Eyes on your textbook, Louisa."

"Sorry. I was just wondering if your co—"

"Ah-ah-ah. If your question isn't related to landform regions, save your wondering until after class."

I couldn't even be concerned about her without getting into trouble. It was her coughing that distracted me in the first place. *Not fair! Maybe she should stay home when she's not feeling well. Maybe she should just stay home forever.* I swallowed a growl that I really, really wanted to let loose.

"Louisa, are you staying on task?"

I jerked. Maybe Mrs. Snyder was turning into a mind reader after all. Lowering my head, I slid my bookmark under the next line. "Yes, Mrs. Snyder. Fully and completely on task."

\* \* \*

Finally, the reading torture ended. I was nowhere near finished the two paragraphs, but I didn't care. If I'd had to read one second longer, that swallowed growl would have exploded from me.

We dragged our desks into a square so we could work on our group project. I sat across from Lexie, and Sophia Wabash faced Nakessa. We each had one part of the project to complete. My job was the map. I carefully pulled it from a plastic sleeve Mom had given me. "I still have to label it, but it'll be done by the deadline." I'd been delaying the labeling. My printing is so messy, even I have trouble reading it sometimes.

"Woah, Louisa." Sophia Wabash dropped her pencil on the desk. "That's really amazing. Your drawings look professional."

I blushed. "Thanks. I thought it would be a cool idea to include illustrations for each region. Once I'm done all of them, I'll color them in."

"I can't believe you did those yourself." Sophia

Wabash slid the map onto her desk, leaning over it, she ran her finger lightly across the polar bear. "The fur looks real."

"You're going to get us an *A+* on our project." Nakessa raised her hand and we high-fived.

"You're a natural." Lexie smiled at me.

"Ah, you guys!" I laughed, not so secretly loving the attention. "Getting an *A+* on a project would be a first for me."

"That's what you get when your mom's an amazing artist. It's in your genes." Nakessa said.

"Ohhh." Sophia Wabash crossed her arms across her chest. "Not fair."

I frowned. "What do you mean?"

"Well, being artistic runs in your family, so drawing is easier for you than the rest of us."

I yanked the map back. "I worked hard on those drawings."

"I didn't mean to hurt your feelings. It's just that I'd have to work way harder than you to get that good."

Heat rushed up my neck. "Welcome to my life. Reading and printing and math aren't exactly easy for me."

"Oh." Sophia Wabash's olive-green eyes grew wide, reminding me of small lily pads. Pink splotches dotted her cheeks "I-I didn't know..."

"Regular stuff that's simple for you takes me

a lot longer. Sometimes it seems impossible and then other stuff like art, is way easier."

"I-I didn't know..."

I shrugged. "It's okay." But it wasn't really. My Less Lou/More Lexie day had tired me out too much to go into a huge explanation of how my brain worked differently.

Then the bell rang.

"Woohoo!" Nakessa and I cheered at the same time.

"Louisa," Mrs. Snyder called over the sounds of twenty-eight fifth graders pulling their desks and chairs across the room. "Please stay after school. I'd like to chat."

"B-but, what about Nakessa? She cheered too, and—" I didn't bother finishing. Mrs. Snyder began wiping the whiteboard. Apparently, cleaning the classroom was more important to her than anything I had to say. "I can't do anything right," I muttered.

"Sorry, Lou," Nakessa said.

What could I have possibly done wrong now? I walked with the Bendables to the doorway, wishing I could leave too. "Lexie, couldn't you use your wand and cast some sort of magic spell on me? I need to be invisible to Mrs. Snyder."

Lexie giggled. "If only." She gave me a big hug. "Just don't talk back."

Nakessa hugged me next. "Be strong and, like Lexie said, don't blurt out anything sassy."

"I never mean to. It just happens."

"Okay, Louisa I'm ready for you," Mrs. Snyder called. "Say good-bye to your friends."

Lexie and Nakessa waved as they disappeared into the hall.

I trudged to the front of the room to meet my doom.

The Shadow Phantom sat down, closing her eyes for a moment. When she opened them again, she looked tired—really tired.

"Are you okay, Mrs. Snyder?"

"That's very kind of you to ask, Louisa." She coughed into her elbow. "I must admit I've felt better. This cold of mine doesn't seem to want to leave. Quite happy it's Friday and I have the weekend to recover." She leaned forward in her chair. "Take a seat, Louisa."

I sat at Little Jack's desk. Sweat dribbled from my armpits.

"Do you know why I asked you to stay?"

I clenched my trembling hands together under the table. I shrugged. "Not really."

"I wanted to let you know I was watching you today."

My entire body stilled. Pretty sure even my heart stopped beating.

"And I liked what I saw."

I slumped forward across Little Jack's desk. I exhaled as if I'd been holding my breath under water for an entire year. "You did?"

"Yes. I could see how hard you were trying to stay on task today."

"You could?"

"It looked exhausting."

My mouth fell open. How did she know it had zapped every ounce of my energy?

"In fact, watching you made me feel even more tired than I already am."

"Oh. I'm sorry. I didn't—"

"Louisa, you—" She coughed again. Her face reddened with each cough. She slumped back in her chair, laying hand on her chest and winced.

"You sound really bad."

"I certainly do." Her laugh caught in her throat, morphing into a rumbling cough. Finally, it stopped. Sweat dotted her nose. "What I wanted to say was keep up the good work. I know it's hard, but just remember, I'm watching."

"Oh...great." *She's always watching. No pressure then.*

"Have a good weekend, Louisa. Get lots of rest. We're starting a new science unit next week. I expect extraordinary things from you."

Extraordinary things? In science? What could

that possibly mean?

She stood, smiling at me.

I tried to smile back, I really did, but my brain was overheating trying to figure out what about me was extraordinary. Instead my smile wobbled and melted into a grimace. My lips began to tremble. No way was I sobbing in front of her again. I leaped to my feet. "Bye!"

Mrs. Snyder's hacking cough chased me across the classroom.

I didn't look back as I darted to the doorway— like a mouse fleeing a cat. An always-watching Shadow Phantom Cat.

# Chapter 13

# Silliest Man
# on Earth

## (and possibly the moon)

After school I leaned against Mr. Popowich's low chain-link fence, grinning at his latest gnome scene. He'd set up five gnomes around a small circle of rocks in the shape of a fire pit. It took me a few minutes to realize the fisherman gnome's rod had a marshmallow on the end instead of a line and lure. Even with Mr. Popowich's distraction, I still got home in seven and a half minutes—an average amount of time.

My day hadn't been horrible. It hadn't been anywhere close to great either. It was mostly blah. But Fridays are Mom's baking day, so I didn't doddle. Mom says cookies are our reward for a week completed. And boy, did I complete that week.

The moment I walked through the doorway I smelled chocolate. My mouth watered nearly as much as Grammers's drooling basset hound, Velma. When Velma smells her vittles frying, she's one sloppy-doggy-mess. Vittles. That's what Grammers calls Velma's special diet of ground beef and rice. Drooling Velma-style, I raced down the hallway to the kitchen. No mom, but in the middle of the kitchen table sat a stack of my favorite chocolate chip cookies. Even baked with tofu, they're still delicious. A sheet of drawing paper perched on top, with a message:

"Have three. No more. I'm taking a nap." Below the note, she'd drawn me, scarfing down cookies. Chocolate covered my face and hands. Crumbs flew everywhere.

I dropped the note, then slumped onto a chair. Elbow on the table, I rested my chin on my hand. I flicked Mom's note. Something deep inside my chest ached. I wanted Mom. All to myself. The baby wasn't even born yet, and it was already hogging all of her attention.

The front door creaked open. "Hello, Nadine! Lou!" Dad called. "I'm home!"

# The U-nique Lou Fox

"Dad!" I leapt up, bumping the table. Tofu cookies slid off the plate. I raced from the kitchen, down the hall, and pitched myself into his arms.

"Wow! Are you happy to see me or what?" He scuffled my hair.

"I'm super happy. Mom's sleeping. I had a weird day."

"Me too. How about we dish over cookies and milk." He rested his hand on my shoulder as we walked to the kitchen.

"Dish?"

"Yes, it means to share stories."

I laughed. "All right, then let's do the dishes."

"That," Dad laughed, leaning against the kitchen counter, "is not what you say!"

He laughed so hard, he tooted. Then he laughed even harder. Tears streamed down his cheeks as he opened the fridge door. Grinning, I sat at the table. My dad is quite possibly the silliest man on earth. Baby d'Artagnan didn't know how lucky he or she was.

Mom stepped into the kitchen. "I'm so happy you're both home. I slept the entire afternoon." She pulled her flowery bathrobe tighter around her middle. It looked snugger than normal.

"When's your stomach going to get super big?" I dipped my third cookie into a glass of milk.

"I'm only two months along, so not for a while."

She patted her slightly rounded stomach. "Although I don't remember getting a bump this early with you."

"Don't they say that women show a lot quicker with their second baby?" Dad asked.

"At this rate Paul, I'm not going to fit through the doorway."

Dad kissed her on the forehead. "Nadine, my love, you look beautiful."

I reached for cookie number four. A slow smile spread across my face as I watched my parents. Nakessa thinks its gross when her parents get all lovey-dovey, but I think my parents are the absolute cutest.

Mom pulled a chair next to me and sat. "I need a big hug."

I dropped my cookie mid-dunk. It sank to the bottom of my glass. When I wrapped my arms around Mom, she made this tiny *oof* sound. I gasped, pulling away. "Did I squish the baby? Did I hurt him—or her?"

"Not in a thousand years could you hurt a fly. Now get back here. I need a Lou top-up."

I hugged her again, but not quite as fiercely. This Four Musketeers thing was going to take some getting used to. Not that I didn't want the baby to come, I just really liked having Mom and Dad all to myself.

# Chapter 14

# Lazy Weekend

**W**e slept later than normal on Saturday morning. Maybe Mom's need for sleep was catching. At 11:00 a.m. I stumbled out of bed and tiptoed into my parents' room. I crawled over their covers and fell asleep between them until noon. All day we lazed around the house. I drew, worked on the play, and listened to *The Book Scavenger* on my e-reader. Mom and Dad tidied up the mess Mom had made in the storage room when she was searching for her lucky maternity clothes.

Sunday was a lot like Saturday, but before bed on Sunday night an amazing idea for our play hit me. It came from something Mrs. Muswagam had mentioned. I wanted to make an enormous change to *The Haunting at Lakeside School*. We needed more actors and they needed to be ant-sized. A whole colony of ants. And ghosts—a whole graveyard full of ghosts.

I glanced over to the *Come From Away* poster above my dresser. It's my all-time favorite play. Even though the whole story is about a tragedy, the songs are so uplifting that the audience leaves the theater feeling hope and not despair. One day I'm going to write like that. I closed my eyes and imagined what it must feel like rushing onto the stage at the end of a play and bowing with all the actors. I looked at the poster again. It took those playwrights five years to write *Come From Away*. I had only a few days to write *The Haunting of Lakeside School* for the talent show.

# Chapter 15

# Perfect Plan in Place

I was the first one to our oak tree Monday morning. I could hardly wait to talk to the Bendables about my big idea. Grabbing a branch, I swung myself up and over the lowest tree limb. Sitting with my back against the trunk, I stretched my legs in front of me. Bending forward, I easily touched my forehead to my knees. Might as well keep flexible while I waited.

"Hey, Lou!" Lexie called.

My head popped up.

She and Nakessa were racing across the

field toward me. Nakessa's thick caramel-colored striped sweater billowed as she ran. It was her favorite Dad-sweater.

Lexie did a cartwheel, followed by a front walkover. Was there anything she couldn't do? She couldn't direct a play. I smiled. That was all mine.

"We...almost didn't see...you up there," Nakessa huffed. Holding her side, she bent over. "Wooooh."

I twirled around the branch, landing on my feet. "I wanted to talk to you about the play. I had this really good idea. What do you think about entering the play in the talent show?"

"That is your best idea. Ever!" Nakessa said.

"Agreed," Lexie said.

A warm ball of happiness bounced through my body. This is why I was best-friend gifted. "Great! Now, to make the biggest splash at the talent show, we need to think big."

"How big?" Nakessa knotted her two braids together under her chin.

"I-ah..." I couldn't take my eyes off Nakessa's braid beard. I dragged my eyes away to look directly at Lexie. "We need to go **enormous**." I grabbed my backpack and slipped out my play book. I flipped to the new pages. "I haven't got it all written, just some notes, but what do you think of more ghosts?"

"Love it," Lexie said.

"Me too," added Nakessa.

"Great! We need to get more kids involved. We can practice every recess, so we'll be ready…. And what do you think about…" I did a drumroll with my fingers on the binder. "…singing ants!"

"Singing ants." Nakessa squeezed my hand. "Are you talking about a musical!?"

Lexie cringed. "Please, no."

Nakessa ignored her. "And do you want a full chorus? That would mean a lot more kids."

"Yeah, I thought we could ask the whole class."

"Do you really think we have enough time to get the play ready?" Nakessa asked. "It's just over a week away."

"I'm pretty sure we do. You two already know most of your lines. We'll keep it simple for everyone else."

"Then I say, yes!" Nakessa pumped her fist high. Her braid beard wobbled.

"Lexie?" I poked her bicep. "What about you?"

"I guess. But I **do not** want to be an ant." She crossed her arms.

"You won't be. You get to stay the hero."

"And I won't sing. Not one note."

"Okay." I crossed my fingers. *Please say yes.*

"And will I still get to use my magic wand?" Lexie really wanted the conditions spelled out.

"Of course. Your wish is my command."

"Careful what you wish for...." Lexie grinned.

"Yeah, yeah, yeah." At that very moment, I was pretty sure everything in my life was nearly perfect. Which was important. I had to get as close to Lexie-perfect as possible with a new baby on the way. On top of being naturally cute, babies need a lot of attention. I needed everything about me to be so amazing that Mom wouldn't totally forget about me. "Okay. The story we've been acting out so far is about a school, haunted by a ghost—the dead principal. And that ghost is you, Nakessa. The hero—you Lexie—is a student with secret magical powers and has to turn the ghost good. Right?"

They nodded.

"But for the talent show, we need to think bigger. What if the ghost principal captures all the students and possesses them? That will make it way harder for our brave hero. We'll keep everyone's lines to a minimum, if any at all. That way there won't be much to memorize."

Lexie smiled. "I like it."

"I *looooooove* it!" Nakessa whooped. "Hey! What if the possessed kids have to do my evil ghostly bidding." She waggled her fingers, "**Booooooh!**"

Lexie laughed. "Good one."

"Maybe..." I bristled a bit. Why did she have to keep trying to take over my job? "Just leave it to me—your fearless director.

# Chapter 16

# Old-lady Winks.
# Shivers.

As soon as the bell rang, we ran to the gym to add our names to the talent show list.

"How many people have signed up?" I asked, as Nakessa added *The Haunting at Lakeside School* to the sign-up sheet on the bulletin board.

Lexie did a quick count. "Fourteen."

"*Everyone's going to loooooove our plaaaaaay!*" Nakessa sang, and as we turned down the hallway to our classroom, Mrs. Snyder's cough bounced off the lockers.

"Wow," Lexie said. "Mrs. Snyder sounds really sick."

"Good," I mumbled.

"What did you say?" Lexie stopped walking.

"Uhm, I just mean if she was really, really sick, she would stay home, and she wouldn't pick on me." Heat rushed up my neck.

Lexie placed her hands on her hips. She gave me her best Lexie Chan are-you-serious look. I squirmed under her glare, suddenly finding the glistening gray floor tiles very interesting. Most likely because those tiles weren't judging me.

"Yikes, I'm outta here." Nakessa pushed past us, into the classroom.

Sadly, staring at the floor didn't stop Lexie.

"Lou," she said. "Mrs. Snyder is old, like—really old. Old people don't do sick well."

"I guess."

Lexie's stare bore into the back of my head all the way into class, across the room, and to our desks. She kept staring at me even after I sat down.

I spun to face her. "What?!"

Lexie jumped in her seat.

"Lou!" Nakessa gasped behind me.

Suddenly my face flamed even hotter than my neck. I hadn't meant to shout. It just sort of burst from my lips. To be honest, I was a bit growly too.

In less than a second, I felt sorry—sorry to the depths of my soul, sorry. Sorry, like you can only be when you yell at one of your very best friends in the entire world sorry. I leaned across the aisle toward Lexie. "I'm so—"

Mrs. Snyder clapped her hands, interrupting my apology. Everyone stared at her. She pointed at me. Of course. Then in a very Shadow Phantomy way, she inched her finger at me. "Come," she mouthed.

My entire body trembled. I stood, expecting my legs to buckle. Fortunately, my limbs are exceedingly strong due to all my Cirque du Soleil practicing. I remained upright. Falling in class would be the most embarrassing thing I possibly could have done. At least since I screamed at Mrs. Snyder last week.

Lexie grabbed my hand. "Don't argue," she whispered. "No sass."

Another heatwave surged up my neck, burning across my cheeks. Even after I'd barked at her, Lexie was being kind to me. Gulping, I took the first shaky step toward the doom at the front of the room.

"Louisa," Mrs. Snyder said quietly, in an oddly breathy voice. Her gray face looked even sicker than on Friday. "I'd like you to start the day as you mean to carry on."

I frowned. I wasn't sure what she meant. She must've realized I was confused, because then she told me loud and clear what she wanted me to do.

"Begin this day with your best foot forward and keep that in mind as the day progresses. I'd like to see more of what you showed me on Friday." She coughed into her elbow, then placed her hands on her chest, wincing. Sweat poured down her face. She grabbed a tissue and wiped her forehead.

"O-okay." I stepped back. She looked like she had the plague.

"Back to your desk, please."

As I walked to my seat, Mrs. Snyder spoke quietly. "Class, I'm feeling unwell, so I'll limit my talking. Time to journal. Today's topic is: How does where we live in the country affect how you see the world? Tell me about how it impacts your daily life. What you do after school. You could tell me about the sports that you play or what your family does on the weekend. Let your imaginations run wild." Mrs. Snyder looked at me, and as if in slow motion, she tilted her pale face and, scrunching one eye, she winked.

**Winked.**

A million tiny wrinkles branched out from her eye to her temple. Monstrous, villainous wrinkles. My breath caught in my throat. What did the wink mean? Was I in trouble before we even started? My stomach flip-flopped. My brain scrambled, thinking of what Mrs. Snyder had said to me. Start the day as I meant to carry on, with my best foot forward. Be more like I was on Friday when I was less Lou and more Lexie.

I glanced over at Lexie. She'd already pulled out her journal. Rustling around in my desk, I tugged out a stack of notebooks. I flipped through them, smacking my journal on my desk. Of course, the journal hit the desk way louder than I had intended. Everyone looked at me. I didn't dare look at Mrs. Snyder. I didn't need to. I could feel her beady eyes watching me. Just like she had promised on Friday. I flipped open my journal and laid my stubby pencil on a fresh page. *How does living here...*

Wait. What was the question?

"*Psst*, Lexie," I whispered, but remembered, if I was to be more like Lexie, I wouldn't need to ask her to help me. I frowned. Being Lexie and me at the same time was confusing.

*Living on the prairie...*

The prairie. Well. The land was flat. Duh. There were loads of farms. Farms had crops. Wheat and...canola? Fields and fields of grain. And they used those big machines to harvest. Tractors? They probably had a fancier name....

That's when I began to wonder what riding a tractor would be like. Would it be like driving a car? How fast could it go? Some of Dad's ancestors had been farmers in Portage la Prairie. What if Dad had become a farmer? Then I would be a farm girl!

I began to doodle.

Which I now realize I should not have done.

Very quickly my doodle turned into a sketch. Time slipped by. My page filled with a field of swaying wheat. Farmer Dad was driving a tractor, and in the far distance along the horizon, were hay bales. I'd drawn me doing a back bend between two of them. Cirque du Soleil Farmer Lou. Fluffy clouds dotted the sky.

A shadow crossed my page. I looked up. Mrs. Snyder stared back. She tapped her red pen on the tractor's front tire. My head dropped. Caught off task. Again.

* * *

When the bell rang, I was totally expecting Mrs. Snyder to make me miss recess again. I was wrong. In fact, she didn't even look up from her desk. She was too busy flipping through papers. In case she suddenly remembered she wanted to wreck my day, I raced from the room and waited for Lexie and Nakessa down the hall by the water fountain. Lexie slowed as they got closer to me.

"Lexie, I'm really, really sorry," I stepped toward her. "I didn't mean to shout at you."

Lexie shrugged. "I guess."

Nakessa stepped between us. "You two need to let bygones be bygones. You need to shake on it."

I held out a trembling hand. A moment of dread filled me. Nausea swirled in my belly. What if... what if Lexie wouldn't shake my hand?

Lexie smiled and pulled me in for a hug. "I can't stay mad at you, Lou."

"You have no idea how scared I was." I squeezed her tight. The gurgling in my tummy settled down.

"*What would we do, without you... Louuuuubadoooo...there's no one quite like yoooouuuuuu!*" Nakessa fluttered her hands in a final flourish.

Laughing, the three of us linked arms and tore out the doors to the field behind the school. Our oak tree, gymnastics, and play rehearsal awaited us.

# Chapter 17

# Double Trouble

"Careful, Lou," Lexie said as I crashed into her for the third time.

"Sorry!" The dread of returning to class and more of Mrs. Snyder's wrinkly winks stirred up butterflies in my stomach. Those butterflies made my handstands wobble, and I kept bashing into Lexie, who smashed into Nakessa.

"Let's just work on the play," Nakessa suggested, as she brushed dirt off her jeans.

"Good idea," I agreed.

"I'll get you, you nasty kid!" Nakessa shouted,

acting like the ghost principal. She chased Lexie around the tree.

I glanced over my shoulder at the school. Maybe Mrs. Snyder had realized she let me go for recess. Would she start lecturing me the moment I stepped one baby toe into the classroom? How was I ever going to—

Lexie cartwheeled on the grass right in front of me, blocking the school from view. "Earth to Lou, where are you?"

Nakessa followed Lexie with a front walkover. "You've drifted...bad."

"I'm sorry. It's just—"

**Brrrriiinng!**

Betrayed by the bell, I trudged across the field. Kids pushed past me, through the doors, and down the hallway. The butterflies in my stomach flapped like wild turkeys. The closer I got to the classroom, the faster they fluttered. With a deep breath, I scurried into the room, hoping to get to my desk without Mrs. Snyder noticing me. I kept my eyes on the floor, ignoring the loud whispers that surrounded me. In seconds flat I reached my desk. Relief washed over me. The Shadow Phantom had not croaked out my name. Only once I sat down, did I dare glance up. Mrs. Muswagam stood smiling at the front of the room. What was our principal doing here?

"Good morning, grade five," she said.

"Good morning, Mrs. Muswagam," we replied.

Lexie passed me a handful of Sweet Tarts.
I popped two in my mouth. Sweet tang zinged my tongue.

"Mrs. Snyder went home sick, so I get to be your teacher. Hopefully, she'll be back tomorrow."

This was the best news I'd heard all year—No! All century! "Woo—" I cheered.

"Lou!" Lexie hissed, cutting off my *hoo*. "Stop it."

I glanced at Lexie. She frowned at me. "Don't be mean."

I peeked back at Nakessa, who dropped her gaze.

"Lou," Mrs. Muswagam said.

Heat flared across my cheeks, as I turned to her. "Yes?" I squeaked.

"I need an assistant. Will you please come up here?" It was one of those questions that teachers ask, that isn't really a question. And this was the principal. A unique principal, but still a principal.

"*Ooooh*, Lou's in trouble again," Big Jack whispered. "Here comes double trouble."

Easing myself out of my seat, I glared at him. I very, very badly wanted to growl at him, I gritted my teeth to stop myself and inched up the aisle.

"No one's in trouble, Jack, unless you keep teasing other students," Mrs. Muswagam said.

"I simply need someone with Lou's imagination to help me with the art lesson."

My head popped up. My jaw relaxed. On top of being unique, she had incredibly good hearing. **In-hu-man-ly** good hearing. She might possibly be an actual alien. I full-on smiled as I bounded to the front of the room. Mrs. Snyder had never once asked me to help.

That's when I made the biggest mistake of my life. I looked out the window at our oak tree and made a wish. I wished that Mrs. Snyder would never return to school.

# Chapter 18

# Unexpected Fear

At lunch, Mr. Diaz sat on a stool at the front of the room. On the whiteboard behind him he had written the Portuguese word of the day. *Obrigado*. Thank you.

"What did your mom pack for lunch today?" Lexie asked. She popped a red grape into her mouth.

"Store-bought cookies."

"Woah!" Lexie raised her hand. I high-fived her.

"Yup. Apparently, pregnancy makes her crave certain foods."

"You're lucky her cravings are tasty." Nakessa shivered. "My mom craved raw garlic, spinach, and lemon juice when she was pregnant with both my sisters. She stuffed it all into a blender and drank it."

"Ew," Lexie said. "That's so gross."

I clapped my hands. "Okay, so back to the play. As your fearless playwright-slash-director, I think I should ask the class to join our play, right now. We need time to practice for the talent show."

Nakessa gave me a thumbs-up. "Go for it."

I raised my hand. "Mr. Diaz, can I speak to the class?"

"Of course."

"Obrigado."

Mr. Diaz smiled. "*Perfeita pronúncia.*" Perfect pronounciation. That didn't surprise me. After all, I am a bit of a parrot. What surprised me was that I understood what Mr. Diaz said.

On the way to the front of the room, I purposely did not look at Big Jack. My feelings still stung from his double-trouble comment. "Hey, everyone! As you know, Nakessa, Lexie, and I write plays. Well, I-I write them...really...and w-we..." I looked out across the class. My heart skipped a beat. Every last person stared back at me. They were so quiet. How did teachers do this every day? I folded my hands in front of me, to stop them shaking. "And, uhm—and as you know, the talent show is coming up in two weeks. We were thinking, uhm..." My mouth dried to dust. I looked at my friends. Lexie smiled huge. Nakessa gave me a thumbs-up. Their eyes grew wider than I'd ever seen. *Oh, no. They look scared—for me!*

I forced more words from my mouth. "We'd like to enter our play..." My tongue stuck to the roof of my mouth. "...and we need..." I couldn't continue. Every drop of saliva had evaporated. Speaking became physically impossible.

Lexie stood up at her desk. "We need a lot more actors, so if anyone's interested, come meet us under the oak tree as soon as lunch is done."

I raced back to my seat. My face burned. Tears stung my eyes. Plunking into my seat, I grabbed my water bottle. I gulped like I had been lost in the desert for ten—no—one hundred years. I thumped my forehead on my desk. I couldn't believe it. I had stage fright.

\* \* \*

After we finished eating, the Bendables stood under our tree, surrounded by nearly the entire fifth grade class. I turned my back to their staring eyes, pulling Nakessa and Lexie close. "What if I freak out again?" I panic-whispered. My heart pounded hard in my chest.

"You won't. It's less stressful out here." Lexie's voice was all calm and soothing, very Mom-like.

"But I might."

"No, you'll be good," Nakessa whispered. "We're under our oak tree. This is our turf. You're going to be fine."

"I could do the talking, if you want." Lexie laid a hand on my shoulder.

"No, that's okay. I'm the director. I'm supposed to be fearless." I spun around and clenched my binder tight to my chest, hoping it would hide my trembling arms. *I am fearless. I am fearless. I am fearless.* I chanted that silently. Obviously. Repeating it out loud would make me appear—not surprisingly—fear**ful**. "Thank you all for coming." I scanned the ocean of fifth graders. Big Jack stared back. My breath caught. "I just have to chat with Lexie and Nakessa for one more teeny, tiny second."

The three of us scurried to the other side of the tree trunk.

"What's wrong? Are you freezing up again?" Lexie whispered.

"No!" I exhaled loudly, needing to calm down. "Not exactly. There's just a lot of kids."

Nakessa peered around the tree. She counted under her breath. "Twenty-two. Is that too many?"

"No, that's no big deal. It's just—"

"Hey!" Big Jack called. "What's taking so long?"

I peeked around the tree. "Just a second. We're...sorting out roles for the whole cast."

A cast. I had my very first, real cast! Excitement raced through me like electricity, zapping away my nerves and clearing my mind. "Okay. Half the class can be a whole colony of singing ants who help the hero. The other half get possessed by the ghost."

"That works," said Lexie.

"It'll be super easy because I won't have to write any new lines for them." Another great idea blasted into my brain. "And Sophia Wabash can be the Ant Queen. I'll give her just a few lines. No problemo."

"But wait. I want to sing. Can't I switch and be the Ant Queen instead?" Nakessa asked.

"I think Sophia Wabash looks more like the Queen Ant," Lexie said. "She's so tall."

"I'm not exactly short." Nakessa kicked a stone.

"I know, but you and Lexie are the leads in the play, which is way better," I explained. "You already know lots of your lines. Without you, there is no story. Nakessa, you get to take over the entire school. I mean, that's a pretty big deal."

Nakessa shrugged. "I guess."

Geez. Talk about a fussy actor. Being a

director was way harder than I imagined. Way harder than writing the play itself!

"What if Lou gave you a song?" Lexie said.

"What?" Why couldn't Lexie just leave the details to me? "I don—"

Nakessa got down on one knee, clasping her hands. "I am begging you. Let me sing!"

"Fine. You can be a singing ghost."

Little Jack poked his head around the tree. "Are you ready yet?"

"Are we going to talk about this play, or what?" Big Jack demanded, pushing past Little Jack.

"Hey!" Little Jack's hands balled into fists.

That is the moment I had the *best* play idea of the day, or possibly my entire life. I would write a new role for Big Jack. I'd show him double trouble. I'd show him I did not like-like him—not in the least. I grinned, trying to look evil. If I hadn't been holding the play binder, I would've rubbed my hands together in a very villainy way. And if I were the villain, I could definitely growl at him. Because I was the playwright after all. Big Jack had no idea, but his new role involved cleaning toilets.

# Chapter 19

# Time Flies

That day, I got home in a typical seven and a half minutes. What wasn't typical was Dad's car parked out front. He never got home before me. The moment I walked in the house, a funny smell hit me—sort of sweet, but mostly burned.

Dad's face popped out of the kitchen at the end of the hall. "Hi! I'm home early."

"Yeah, I can see that." I sniffed. "Are you cooking something?"

"Well, I'm burning something. I need your help."

"Sure." Wisps of smoke tickled my nose and

stung my eyes, as I walked toward Dad. The closer I got to the kitchen, the less I could smell any sweetness at all. Only smouldering food. "It really stinks in—" I stopped in the kitchen doorway. A huge bag of flour lay tipped on its side, and flour spilled from the counter onto the floor. Dirty measuring cups filled the sink. Worst of all, the fridge door stood wide open. Mom would hate that. Very bad for the environment. I looked at Dad. He was wearing Mom's #1 Earth Mother apron. It looked like he'd spilled every ingredient on Earth on it. "What did you do?"

"Mom wasn't feeling well, so I came home early to make pancakes—another of her cravings." He opened the cupboard under the sink. Burned round discs were piled in the trash can. "I'm still perfecting them."

"Oh, Dad." I shut the fridge door. "Lucky for you, I've made a zillion pancakes with Mom. First things first." That's what she always said when we started baking. "We need a clean work surface."

"Bugaboo, what would I do without you?"

"Starve. Apparently."

\* \* \*

After I rescued Dad and the pancakes, I went to my room to work on the play. I had to figure out how to get everyone included. Plus, I needed songs. With only nine days until the talent show, the songs needed to be easy to learn and remember. I stared at my computer screen. My thoughts drifted back to *Lexie Chan and her Band of Merry Women.* With that play, we'd added our own words to familiar tunes. I could do the same with *The Haunting of Lakeside School.* We had ants and ghosts. Ant songs—

That was it!

I picked up the microphone, singing, "*The Ants Came Marching One By...*" My words flashed on the screen. Lost in composing, I jumped when Mom rested her hand on my shoulder. The hours had flown by.

* * *

That night, both Mom and Dad tucked me in, just like in the olden days before pregnancy.

Mom sat next to me, smoothing my hair off my face. "When you're snuggled up for bed, you look like my sweet little baby. I remember when we brought you home from the hospital. You were so tiny."

"How big was I?" I knew the answer. She'd told me a million times.

"So scrawny—just a skinny little thing. You were

completely bald, and you had these big, dark eyes. And your buddy, Pearl, was longer than you."

"You were smaller than a stuffed piglet," added Dad.

I yawned. My eyelids wanted to close, but I didn't want to fall asleep. Not yet. This was the first night in a long time that Mom had been awake to tuck me in. I wanted this moment to last forever.

Mom started to sing the lullaby she'd made up for me, when I was only a few days old.

*"Momma loves you, Daddy loves you. Don't you know that it's true,*

*Everything that we do, we do just for you.*

*Everything and everyway, Louisa it's true*

*Everything that we do, we do just for you..."*

It's no masterpiece, but it's not every day you get a song written for you. Anyway, I guess I fell asleep, because the next thing I knew, Dad was calling me for breakfast. That's when my whole world changed. Again.

# Chapter 20

# Raging Jealousy

I came downstairs to find a present in the center of the kitchen table with my name scrawled across it in black felt marker. "What is it?" I squeezed the bright blue package as I picked it up. I love trying to guess what's under wrapping paper. "It's soft. Not too big...mitts?"

"Nope, but you can wear it." Mom put her hand on Dad's.

"You're the best guesser." Dad laughed. "Rip off the paper."

I tore it open. "A tie-dye shirt!" I held it up,

blocking my parents faces. White printing covered the front. I read the words slowly. "Big sis..ter times two." I lowered the shirt. Mom and Dad had grins that I wished I could mimic, but my quivering lips wouldn't smile. I was too...stunned...shocked... **stu-pe-fied**. A five-dollar word, but not quite right to describe my feelings. Maybe because I'd never felt like I did at that moment before. Nausea gurgled in my belly. My eyes stung.

"Do you know what it means?" Mom asked.

"Uhm, I think so."

"Two d'Artagnans!" Dad said. "Twins!"

"Twins. Super. Okay." *No way can I compete against two babies. I'll never get any time with Mom ever again.* Grabbing the shirt, I pushed away from the table, raced down the hall, up the stairs, into my bedroom, and slammed the door. With all my might, I twisted the shirt. I wanted to rip it to shreds. But since I'm not Hulk-strong, I just got angrier.

So much angrier.

"**Aaaahhhhggg!**" I screamed. "Dumb baby! Dumb **babies**! I wish Mom never got pregnant! I wish those babies ceased to exist!" I threw the shirt across the room. It landed on top of my bookshelf. Good. Dumb shirt.

"Louisa," Mom said, knocking on my door. "Can I come in?"

"No! Leave me alone!" I threw myself on the bed and scrambled under the covers.

"Louisa, it's Dad. Please let us in."

*No kidding it's Dad. Who else would it be?* "Go away!" My voice broke, as I yelled. "I wish—I wish..." but I couldn't continue.

The door flew open. Mom and Dad barged in.

"Oh, Louisa." Tears ran down Mom's cheeks.

They both crawled onto the bed. Dad squeezed in between me and the wall and wiped my tears. Mom lay on the other side of me, stroking my cheek.

Slowly, I calmed down. We snuggled past the morning bell at school. We snuggled until my jealous rage wore itself out. Jealousy, that's the feeling I couldn't name. I despised it as much as I despised English class. Maybe more.

Mom and Dad walked me to school. It was like being little again. I loved it.

"Louisa, remember. We could have two hundred babies, and we'd still love you." Mom squeezed my hand.

"Although we'd need a much bigger house for that many kids," Dad said.

"Oh, Paul." She shook her head. "Louisa, what Dad and I are trying to say is that as parents we have endless love. It's just how we're made."

"I know." I stared at the pavement. "I just felt... you know...jealous."

Being jealous is not a wonderful feeling. It's **mis-er-a-ble**, in fact. A five-dollar-word for sure, and miserable is sad times a million, and jealousy churns in your tummy making you feel sick. Apparently it can send a person into an angry rage. I wanted nothing more to do with jealousy.

"We know." Dad kissed the top of my head. "Anything else you want to talk about before we go inside?"

I hesitated. I really hoped they hadn't heard me say that stuff about the babies—about wishing Mom had never gotten pregnant. If they had, surely they would have mentioned it. And what they didn't know couldn't hurt them. Or me. "No, I'm good."

We entered the school and went straight to the office. Mrs. Muswagam stood behind the counter talking to the secretary. The moment she saw us, she smiled right up to her eyes. "Louisa, we were getting worried about you. You're never late."

"Our fault," Dad said. "Cross my heart, we'll unlock her cage earlier tomorrow."

"Dad!" Sometimes he was silly at the wrong times.

Mrs. Muswagam laughed. "I see where Louisa gets her sense of humor."

Dad and Mom each gave me a hug. "I'll see you after school," Mom whispered in my ear.

"Remember what we said. We've enough love for two hundred babies."

"See you tonight, Louisa." Dad put his arm around Mom's waist, guiding her out of the office.

"Louisa," Mrs. Muswagam said. "Before you head to class, I need to talk to you."

"Oh, okay." I followed her into her office.

"It's about something Mrs. Snyder shared with me."

My shoulders slumped. I hadn't even seen my teacher yet, and I was already in trouble. Mrs. Snyder was the sneakiest of Shadow Phantoms. I sat completely still on the swivel chair and waited, my lips clamped shut.

"Mrs. Snyder wanted to talk to you herself, but she's away sick today and will likely be gone for the rest of the week. Fingers crossed she'll be back next week."

My head popped up. Two days Shadow Phantom free—and possibly a week! I'd wished her away and **poof**! Gone.

**Poof**.

That meant that I wouldn't have to concentrate on not getting in trouble all day long until my brain felt like it would explode.

"Mrs. Snyder organized the next professional development day for all the teachers," Mrs. Muswagam said.

I tried hard to keep listening, but all I could think about was how awesome the rest of the week would be. I knew Mr. Diaz couldn't be our substitute teacher, but maybe it would be someone like him—someone who wouldn't make me miss recess. Someone who wasn't watching my every move. Someone who wasn't a Shadow Phantom with evil wrinkly winks—

"Louisa?" Mrs. Muswagam broke through my thoughts of a Mr. Diaz-style teacher. "Did you hear anything I just said?"

I shook my head. I'd drifted bigger than big.

"Mrs. Snyder is quite ill, but even so, she wanted you—"

The door pushed open. It was the secretary. "I'm so sorry to interrupt, but it's a parent, and it's urgent."

"All right, we'll talk later, Louisa. The substitute teacher will be waiting for you."

I couldn't help myself. I smiled.

Mrs. Muswagam tilted her head. "Something funny?"

"Nope. Not a thing." Which was not a lie. I was **ec-stat-ic**—the perfect five-dollar-word for extreme joy. For all it mattered to me, Mrs. Snyder could stay away forever.

# Chapter 21

# Freckle Dipper

As soon as I was out of sight of the office, I raced down the hallway and whizzed by the fourth-grade class. The teacher shouted after me, "Walking! No running!"

I slowed to an incredibly speedy fast-walk, eager to get to class. Eager. Me! Louisa Elizabeth Fitzhenry-O'Shaughnessy couldn't wait to get to class. I'm not going to lie. Eager felt amazing—as amazing as when you've finished a floor routine in gymnastics. You've landed your last front flip—your arms up are up high,

and your face is one **gi-nor-mous** smile. Eager
for me felt a whole lot like that. Only better.
I couldn't help myself. I entered the classroom
and drawled, cowboy-style, "Howdy pardners."

A woman stopped writing on the whiteboard
and turned to me.

"Sorry, to be tardy, Ma'am." I tipped an
imaginary hat at the substitute teacher.

"You must be Louisa Elizabeth," she replied.

"The one and only, but you can call me Lou."
I did a fancy bow like actors do at the end of a play.

Everyone giggled.

"And I'm the one and only Miss Tesoro." She
slid her navy-blue blazer off and draped it across
the back of Mrs. Snyder's chair. "You're just as
I expected."

"Oh." Just as she expected? I didn't have a
clue what that meant.

"Please take your seat. Lateness is no excuse
for falling behind your classmates." She smiled
again. Her white teeth glistened. That's when
I noticed something that made my stomach lurch.
Even though her cheeks dimpled, her smile did
not reach her eyes.

With my head down, I scurried to my seat.

"Louisa Elizabeth, the class is journaling until
morning recess. I've written today's topic on the
board."

"It's Lou," I mumbled, glancing at the whiteboard. Black printing covered nearly every square inch. Only a tiny white border remained. "That's the whole topic? It's so long."

"Yes. It is," replied Miss Tesoro. She raised her perfectly sculpted eyebrows, tapping the whiteboard marker on her hand. "Time to get started."

I reached into my desk and grabbed my journal.

"*Psst.* Lou," Nakessa tapped me on the shoulder. "Are you okay?"

I turned in my seat. "Yeah."

Nakessa frowned at me "You're late. You're never late," she whispered. You could've fit a second Nakessa in her dad's massive Jets hockey hoody. She'd rolled the sleeves up so many times, the cuffs looked like wrist bands.

"I had a bumpy morning. I—"

"Girls, talking is **not** working. Louisa Elizabeth, get to work. Keep your eyes on your own journal. Focus, Louisa Elizabeth."

*Louisa Elizabeth. Louisa Elizabeth. Louisa Elizabeth.*

Was Miss Tesoro a Shadow Phantom in training? I paged through my journal to the farm scene. Dad looked happy sitting on the tractor. He'd probably just tooted. I giggled and glanced

up at Miss Tesoro, Trainee Shadow Phantom.
She tucked a lock of dark brown hair behind her
ear, then pushed her glasses farther up her nose.
Thankfully, she seemed too busy reading a sheet
of paper at Mrs. Snyder's desk for my giggle to
catch her attention.

I pulled out a black marker and outlined the
tractor wheels. Then something Mrs. Snyder had
said the other day popped right into my mind. It
was from the day when I put my More-Lexie-Less-
Lou plan into action.

*Start the day as you mean to carry on. Put
your best foot forward.*

I looked at Lexie. She was deep in journal
mode. **She** wasn't outlining a sketch that she
wasn't supposed to have drawn in the first place.
Sighing, I put the marker down and flipped the
page. Squinting at the board, I began reading the
first line under my breath, "In your own words,
de..scribe…" Then the words squiggled. I tried to
keep reading, but the sentence made zero sense.
I would've just asked Miss Tesoro, but her eyes
didn't smile, which made her sort of scary and
made me too nervous to raise my hand.

My left arm rested across one side of the
journal. I stared at the freckles on it. Most
were a pale ginger brown, but a few were milk
chocolatey-colored. I tilted my head. It was as if—

There was a pattern in my freckles!

If I only looked at the darker ones, I could totally see the Big Dipper. Just like on my bedroom ceiling. Who knew my arm held a secret map of the cosmos? I grabbed my black pen. Carefully, so I didn't smudge, I pressed down on the darker freckles. Now it was easier to see the gentle slope of the handle, right into the Big Dipper's scoop at the end.

"*Pssst.* Lou," Lexie whispered.

I jumped. My pen slid down my arm. "Geez, Lexie." I whispered back. "You scared me to death."

"What're you doing?"

I twisted my forearm so she could see. "The constellations of course." I pointed to the long dash. "And thanks to you, Halley's Comet."

Lexie giggled. "Show Nakessa."

I looked back at Nakessa, lifting my arm. Nakessa's eyes got wide, she covered her mouth. It didn't stop the deep rumble in her throat.

**Oh. No.**

Silence.

I counted. One, two, three—

**"Haaack!"**

She laugh-barked.

That's when the Bendables got sent to the office.

143

# Chapter 22

# Note to Self: Listen to Talking Eyeballs

**"I** miss Mrs. Snyder," Lexie said as we slowly made our way to the office.

"Me too. Mrs. Snyder gives second chances." Nakessa's eyes were red. I could tell she was trying not to cry.

"Are you kidding?" I said. "My wish came true."

"What do you mean?" Lexie asked.

"About Mrs. Snyder, not coming back to school."

Nakessa stopped walking. "You wished she'd get sick?"

145

"No, not sick. I just wanted her to go away."

"Wasn't it your grandma who said to be careful what you wish for?" Lexie asked.

"Yeah, but it's just wishing, it doesn't mean anything. Grammers is superstitious."

Lexie shrugged. "I guess, but don't you think wishing bad things on other people will bring you bad luck?"

"Luck doesn't exist. That's another silly superstition. You aren't superstitious are you, Nakessa?"

"I wouldn't want to walk under a ladder or break a mirror—stuff like that."

"What about wishes?"

"I'd listen to Lexie and your grandma. Be careful what you wish for."

\* \* \*

The secretary sent us straight into Mrs. Muswagam's office, with me in the lead. I peeked back at Lexie and Nakessa who hovered by the door. Lexie tugged on her ear. Nakessa's normally tawny face paled. She breathed so heavily she sounded like Darth Vader. I'd never heard her sound like that before. She stepped behind Lexie. I was about to say something about space movies, but at that very second Mrs. Muswagam raised her head.

She didn't look happy. She'd never looked so serious. *Uh-oh*.

"Girls." Mrs. Muswagam's voice was as soft and gentle as ever. "Tell me why you're here."

I shrugged. "I think—"

Nakessa jumped out from behind Lexie. Her eyes were huge. "We interrupted the class! We were wrong! Please don't call our parents."

"Do you all feel this way?"

"Yes." Lexie nodded, her voice whisper-quiet.

Mrs. Muswagam turned her attention to me. "And Lou? What about you?"

"I ah..."

Lexie's ear tugging stole my attention from the principal. I glanced over. If Nakessa's eyes were huge, Lexie's were moon-size. If her eyes could speak, they'd be shouting: "Don't talk back. No sass!"

Unfortunately, I ignored their warning. "What happened to second chances?" The moment I spoke, I knew I should've listened to Lexie's eyeballs and kept quiet.

Mrs. Muswagam sighed. "Okay." She turned to my friends. "You two can head back to class. You owe Miss Tesoro an apology. She's new to our school and disruptive behavior is not the first impression we should give her."

Nakessa's breath whooshed out. "Thank you.

Thank you. Thank you."

Lexie nodded like a bobble-head doll. "We'll apologize—we promise."

As my friends left the room, Lexie looked back. She tugged her ear one final time, before disappearing from view.

"Now, Lou," Mrs. Muswagam said. "Please sit."

I slunk into my usual chair, no desire to spin. "Are you going to yell at me?"

She smiled. "Do I seem like a yelling sort of person?"

I tilted my head, thinking about all the times we'd talked. Well, not all the times because there were too many to count. And math and I are not great pals, so...

"Louisa?"

"No."

"Good, because I try very hard not to yell at students. Now, please tell me what happened in class."

"Well, I...I..." What did happen? It was kind of a jumble. "First, I got to the room late. When I sat at my desk, I looked at the board and the assignment and...I didn't really understand what we were supposed to do. I would've asked Miss Tesoro, but she made me nervous, so I started looking at my journal and then..." I held up my arm to show Mrs. Muswagam the Big Dipper and Halley's Comet. "...I got sidetracked by my freckles."

"Oh," Mrs. Muswagam covered her mouth and coughed. "I'll talk to Miss Tesoro and let her know that you may need to ask for clarification with assignments. Next time, just ask for help."

She made it sound so easy.

"I need to share something else with you," Mrs. Muswagam said. She walked over to the meeting table. In her hand was a thick pink file folder. Along the side tab my name was written in thin black marker. She sat opposite me in one of the swivel chairs. "Of all the students in your class, Louisa, you're the one Mrs. Snyder never tires of talking about."

*I bet.* I slumped in the chair, groaning. "Great."

"You're correct. It is great. Really great."

I shot upright.

"I thought that would get your attention." Mrs. Muswagam pulled a page out of the file. She placed it on the table, turning it to face me.

"Hey, that's my sketch of the schoolyard. I did that the first week of school." I couldn't believe Mrs. Snyder had kept it.

"I know. It's breathtaking."

Breathtaking? Only Mom talked about my drawings like that. I blushed. "I guess."

"Mrs. Snyder says you're the most creative

student she's ever taught. In fact, she said that if creativity had a middle name, it would be Louisa. I agree with her assessment of you. You simply ooze imagination."

*Ooze imagination?* My jaw dropped. I bet at that moment I looked like a spitting image of Velma, the basset hound. Only a whole lot less slobbery.

"Does that surprise you?" Mrs. Muswagam's dark eyes twinkled.

"Totally."

Mrs. Muswagam's face suddenly went serious. She didn't frown exactly, but her smile flattened. "But she's also really worried."

"Oh." Mrs. Snyder was still out to get me. It was impossible for her to say anything one hundred percent nice about me. Wishing for anything different was like a hound dog wishing to be—

"Yes, she's worried that she's failing you." Mrs. Muswagam's words karate chopped through my thoughts.

"What's that now, Ma'am?" I was so shocked I slipped into Southern Carolina talk without thinking.

"Oh, Louisa you are too much." She laughed. "Mrs. Snyder knew she didn't understand dyslexia or ADHD enough to help you properly. That really bothered her, so she's arranged for an educational psychologist to speak at the upcoming teachers' professional development day."

"She did that for me?"

"Yes. Mrs. Snyder takes her job very seriously."

"Oh."

"And even though she's as sick as a dog, I know she'll try hard to make it to the session on Friday. Helping you is all she's talked about since September."

"Really?"

Mrs. Muswagam nodded. She tilted her head, watching me. This was impossible. Mrs. Snyder hated me.

"I thought...I thought..." I shook my head, my brainpower slowing to molasses. Which is officially slower than a snail trudging through chunky peanut butter. How had I been so wrong about my teacher? For two months, I'd been all she talked about—in a good way.

Mrs. Muswagam's gentle voice was even softer than usual. "Ahh. You thought she was being too hard on you."

My head jerked. I examined Mrs. Muswagam. She said she wasn't a mind reader, but I wasn't so sure about that. "How did you know?"

"You're a lot like me when I was in school. I had a teacher whom I thought was too hard— mean even. But she only wanted me to be a better student than I thought I was. It sure didn't feel like it at the time, though."

I closed my eyes for a moment, then looked back at Mrs. Muswagam. "Are you dyslexic, too? Do you have ADHD?" I wasn't sure I was allowed to ask the principal that, but I needed to know how she understood me so well.

"No, I just didn't have much self-confidence. I didn't think I was as smart as everyone else."

"But you're a principal."

Mrs. Muswagam laughed. "I wasn't always."

"No, I guess not." I smiled, then my smile turned into a giggle, and soon we were laughing together. A kid principal. The very idea was **ri-dic-u-lous**.

# Chapter 23

# Lou Fox is Stunned

I stood outside the classroom doorway, determined to make this the best apology ever. Taking a deep breath, I walked inside.

Miss Tesoro glanced up. "Good to see you back with us, Louisa Elizabeth."

Louisa Elizabeth. I clenched my fists.

Miss Tesoro stepped toward me. "Louisa Elizabeth, is everything okay?"

"Uh-huh." As my fingernails dug into my palms, I remembered I was supposed to be sorry. I was supposed to be **re-morse-ful**—overflowing with guilt. The problem is, it's nearly impossible to feel remorseful about someone who insists on calling you Louisa Elizabeth, as if it's one long word. I was Lou. Soon to be Lou Fox.

I inhaled, then slowly exhaled, relaxing my hands. I had to be remorseful. I promised Mrs. Muswagam. "Good to see you too, Miss Tesoro." I marched up to her desk. "I wanted to say sorry for earlier—for disrupting the class." My palms began to sweat. I lowered my voice, hoping no one else would hear me. "I know it might not look like it, but I'm actually trying really hard to do better."

Miss Tesoro smiled. This time it reached up to her eyes. "I can see why Mrs. Snyder likes you so much. That was a very kind apology. You may take a seat. We're working on art. In Mrs. Snyder's notes, she said you like that subject."

I nodded my head, Miss Tesoro's words playing over in my mind.

*Mrs. Snyder likes me. So much.*

# Chapter 24

# A Not-so-simple Name Change

The moment we got outside for recess, the Bendables linked arms.

"I've got huge news," I said, as we neared the play structure. "My mom's having twins."

"You're so lucky!" Nakessa said.

"Yeah," said Lexie. "I only have one little brother and my parents aren't having any more kids."

"Lucky. Yup. That's me."

"Hey, are you okay?" Lexie asked, slowing to a stop.

"Yeah, it's just a lot of change all at once."

"Totally, but wait until those little babies arrive," Lexie said. "The second you meet them, you'll love them."

"Sure." I stared at the pavement. I really, really hoped so, but part of me dreaded it. That was something I was sure my friends would never understand. They both loved being big sisters.

"Look!" Nakessa pointed. "The whole cast is waiting for us!"

I looked up. Fifth graders surrounded our oak tree. Now that, I could get excited about. Arms still linked, we charged across the grass.

"Hi everyone," I said, as we reached them. "Thanks again for wanting to take part. Half of you get to be singing ants who help defeat the ghost." I looked at Sophia Wabash. "They're led by a Queen Ant and you're perfect for that role."

"The Queen?" Sophia Wabash grinned. "Thanks, Louisa!"

"You're welcome. The Queen joins forces with the hero and leads the ant colony in a fight against the ghost principal." As I kept talking, I noticed something. My mouth wasn't drying up. I wasn't frozen to the ground. My heart wasn't racing in my chest, like Velma the basset hound's after chasing a tennis ball. "The other half of you are fifth grade students who get possessed by the principal. Oh, and Big Jack, you're the custodian. You get to carry a toilet plunger." A smile crept onto my face. My stage fright had vanished. A thrill zinged through me.

"Woo-hoo!" Cheered Big Jack.

Only Big Jack would be excited by a toilet plunger. "As you know, Lexie's the hero, who's secretly a wizard. She wants to fit in, so she hides her magic until she has to embrace her true magician-self to defeat the ghost."

Everyone started chatting.

"Now cast," I spoke louder, so they could hear me. "I'll count you off as a one or a two. If you're a one, you're a student ghost, so stand over there by Nakessa, the ghost principal. If you're a two, you're an ant and will go stand next to Sophia Wabash.

"And finally, costumes. If you're an ant, wear all black. You need to make pipe cleaner antennas this weekend, so we can do a dress rehearsal on Monday at lunch. If you're a ghost, wear all white, or a bedsheet. Try to find a sheet without a pattern. Keep it simple, people. And Lexie, dress as a typical fifth-grader and don't forget your wand."

"Sounds like you've got everything all figured out," said Nakessa.

"Yeah, like the whole, entire play." Lexie

swooped her homemade magic wand in a circle. "Down to every last costume."

"Yup." I quickly counted off the kids into their groups, skipping over Big Jack.

"Wait, what about me?" he asked. "Where do I stand?"

"By yourself. I don't care where."

Lexie jabbed me in the ribs with her wand. "Lou. Mean!"

I rolled my eyes. "Fine. Go over there by Nakessa." I passed out the songs I'd written for the ghosts and the ants. "I think you'll find the songs easy to remember. Queen Ant, you sing the first verse, solo. Then the ants join in. Once your song is over, Nakessa and the ghosts sing their song."

Sophia Wabash began to sing:

*"The ants came marching two by two, hurrah, hurrah!*
*The ants came marching two by two, to save the school from Mrs. Choo..."*

The other ants joined in.

Nakessa stomped over to me. "You changed my character's name to Mrs. Choo? The ghost was supposed to be Mrs. Kaur. I picked that name."

"I know, but Kaur doesn't rhyme with two."

Nakessa tossed her braids over her shoulders and stood with her legs shoulder-width apart. "Then you should've changed the song."

I frowned. Why was she getting so upset?

"There isn't a lot that rhymes with Kaur, Nakessa. The song needs to be catchy and easy to learn. The talent show is next Tuesday."

"I know that." She crossed her arms. "I signed us up, remember?"

"Of course I remember. I was there with you." My heart began to race. I'd spent a lot of time writing those songs and I didn't want to write new ones. "Why's it such a big deal to change the name?"

"Because this is supposed to be **our** play and it seems like you've taken over everything." Nakessa's waved her arms in the air.

"I'm the playwright **and** the director. Someone's got to be in charge and—"

"Hey, Nakessa," Little Jack called. "It's our turn to sing the ghost song."

"It just would've been nice if you talked to me first," Nakessa said. Her voice quieter than normal.

"I-I'm sorry." I held my play binder close to my chest. Could everyone hear my heart pounding through it?

Nakessa joined the group of ghosts. Together they began to sing the ghost's song to the *London Bridge is Falling Down* tune.

*"Lakeside school is haunted now,*

*haunted now,*
*haunted now.*
*Lakeside School is haunted now!*
*Look out! Or you'll be NEXT!"*

I just wanted the play to be the best it could be. Especially now that I knew how hard Mrs. Snyder had worked for me. Hopefully, she was back at school for the talent show. I needed to prove that I was worth her hard work.

# Chapter 25

# Big Deal

At bedtime, Mom yawned so wide I thought her jaw might actually fall off her face. She covered her mouth. "Sorry. Tired." She waddled across the carpet to my bed. She wore a long sky-blue shirt over navy leggings. One of her lucky outfits. I thought they looked a lot like pajamas.

"I think your belly is growing by the hour," I said, curling around Pearl's fuzzy body.

"Really?" She placed her hands on either side of her bump. "Huh. I think you're right."

Dad kissed me on the forehead. He ran a

finger across what remained of the black marker-stars on my forearm.

I giggled.

"Looks like the Big Dipper will be with you for a few days." Dad shook his head. "Did you get more play written tonight?"

"Yup. I had to write out more stage directions for my cast."

"A cast." He raised his eyebrows and looked at Mom. "Sounds impressive, eh Nadine?"

"It sure does." Mom sat by my feet.

I smiled. "It's only been the Bendables before. Working with so many kids is harder than I thought."

Mom laid a hand on my leg. "You can do it, Louisa."

"I hope so, it's just..." I looked at the constellations on the ceiling. "Nakessa got angry at me today."

"Oh. That doesn't sound like her," Mom said, frowning.

"She's not perfect," I grumbled. *Not everything is my fault.*

Dad pulled Pearl out from under my covers. He bopped the pig's snout on my nose. "No need to snap at your mom."

My eyes darted to her. "Sorry, Mom."

She shook my toes. "It's all right. Tell us what happened."

"I wrote this super ant song and I needed to make it rhyme. To make the rhyme work I had to change the name of Nakessa's character."

Dad shrugged. "Doesn't sound like a big deal. I wonder why it upset her?"

"She said I should've talked to her first. All because she picked her character's name."

"Ah, I see." Mom nodded her head. "Sounds like that was important to her. Names are like that."

"I guess, but I'm sure it's no big deal."

"You know your friend best."

"It'll be fine." But Mom's words kept running through my mind.

*Names are like that.*

Oh, no! Kaur was the name of Nakessa's grandma. The grandma who used to make curry and who died two years ago. The name had to be a big deal for Nakessa. What if it had been Grammers who had died? My stomach churned. I hadn't meant to upset Nakessa.

Mom and Dad kissed me.

"Good night, sleep tight, don't let the bed bugs bite," Dad said.

I forced myself to reply, pretending everything was fine. "But they can't get me, and they can't get you, because..." Dad flicked off my light. Mom closed the door. "...I'm the Mighty Bugaboo," I whispered.

Within moments the constellations glowed down on me. The Big Dipper seemed to shine extra bright.

"Don't judge me. I'm sure it will be fine." Talking to fake stars. Not a good sign.

# Chapter 26

# Un-wishing
# Wishes

**W**hen I got to school the next day, Nakessa was hanging upside down from the lowest branch of our oak tree.

"Hey! Do you want to help me stretch?" I called up to her, hoping she wasn't still mad.

She didn't reply.

Lexie stepped out from behind the tree trunk. She had an open book in one hand, her wand held high in the other.

"Lexie, can you help me?" I asked.

"I'm too busy reading about spells."

"Oh." Strange. She'd never been too busy to stretch before.

I cupped my hand over my eyes to block the sun and looked up. "Is everything okay, Nakessa?"

"Oh, are you still calling me Nakessa?"

I frowned. "What else would I call you?

"I just wondered if you decided to change my name too. How about Emma or Sarah or-or... Henrietta?"

"Henrietta?" Lexie closed the book. "Oh, boy."

Yup. She was still mad. "I-I had to make the name change for the song," I explained.

"You. You. **You**!" Nakessa swung herself upright and jumped to the ground, landing about an inch from me.

I stumbled backward. "I-I'm sorry. Really. I should've thought about your grandma."

Nakessa kicked the ground. A clump of grass flew into the tree trunk.

"Honestly, Nakessa. I forgot. If I had remembered, I never would've changed the name. I'm really, truly, forever sorry. Sorry to Pluto and back."

"That's a pretty good apology," Lexie said, stepping between us. "Let bygones be bygones. You should shake on it."

I held my hand out. I was becoming a pro at messing up with my friends.

"Only if we can secretly keep her name Kaur—for my grandma. Just between us." Nakessa said.

"Of course." I wished I'd thought of that myself.

Nakessa shook my hand.

When the bell rang, we walked into the school behind Little Jack and Sophia Wabash. "Did you hear that Mrs. Snyder's really sick?" Little Jack asked her.

"It's probably pneumonia," Sophia Wabash said, as we passed the library. "My mom's a nurse and she told me old people get it easily."

Pneumonia?

"Is that serious?" Little Jack asked.

"Super serious." Sophia Wabash nodded her head so fast, her curls collided. "Old people die from pneumonia all the time."

"Oh, no!" said Lexie.

I stopped in my tracks.

"You don't think..." Lexie said, staring at me.

Nakessa grabbed my arm, spinning me to face her. "Your wish!"

"No," I whispered. "Impossible."

"You cursed—" Lexie began.

"Our teacher." Nakessa finished.

\* \* \*

All I could think about for the rest of the day was
Mrs. Snyder. Did my wish give her pneumonia?
I wanted to talk to my friends about it, but
I already knew what they thought—I'd cursed our
teacher and made her sick. All this time, Mrs.
Snyder had been trying to find ways to help me
and I was so horrible.

That's when the worst thought of all popped
into my head. What if Mrs. Snyder died? She was
old. Almost ancient. Shame twisted in my belly.
Shame was a feeling way worse than jealousy.
If only I could unwish my wish.

By the time I got home my head felt like
tiny jackhammers were cracking my skull open.
I dropped my bag at the door and dragged my feet
upstairs. Mom served me dinner in bed. I didn't
even stay awake long enough for my parents to
tuck me in.

# Chapter 27

# Worst Day Ever

I woke up in a cranky mood the next day.
I snapped at Mom and Dad at breakfast. At
school, I didn't even meet my friends at our oak
tree. Instead, I snuck inside the school and hid in
a bathroom stall until the bell rang. During class,
I avoided all eye contact with everyone. Who'd
want to talk with a teacher-curser?

At recess, I followed the cast to our oak tree to
practice the play. Within a few minutes, I somehow
got lost in the scene and forgot all about cursing

Mrs. Snyder. Everything went well until we got to Big Jack's line.

Big Jack held a ruler, pretending it was a toilet plunger. "I-um. Don't remember my line."

My back tightened. I'd only given him one line. How hard could that be? "All you say is, "Stop! No!" Just two words. That's it. Simple." Anger flickered in my belly.

"Stop! No!" Big Jack nodded. "Got it."

"Okay," I said, taking a deep breath. I needed to calm down. "We'll begin again at your line, Nakessa."

"Okay. Ready." Nakessa looked around. "I smell more fifth-graders! **Waaahhhaaaa!**"

Little Jack screamed, "Someone help us!"

Big Jack lifted his pretend plunger high in the air. "**Aahhhh!**" He lowered the ruler, frowning. "I—oh. I forgot again."

I rolled my eyes. The flicker of anger caught light. "Ad-lib! Ad-lib! Ad-lib!"

"Huh?" Big Jack frowned. "What's adlibadlibadlib?"

"Ad-lib. It means doing whatever you like, which you're great at. You're a master at saying **anything** that pops into your brain." I was now in a total rage. "In fact, you might be a genius at speaking without thinking."

"Huh?" Big Jack scratched his chin.

"**Double Trouble**! That's what you called me!
Ring any bells??" My face was up against his.

"What are you talking about?"

He had to be acting dumb. "Maybe I should
write **act dumb** into the script for you." A sharp
crackling laugh burst out of me.

He stepped back. "Why're you so mad?"

"Lou! Stop!" Lexie yanked my arm.

I spun to face her. "What?!"

"You're being mean."

"I am not!" I turned to the cast. "Everyone take
five!"

Little Jack frowned. "What's that supposed to
mean?"

Sophia Wabash whispered to him, "We're
supposed to take a five-minute break."

"Amateurs. I'm working with amateurs,"
I muttered. I didn't think anyone had heard me.
I was wrong.

"Yeah—you are. No one here is a professional
actor." Lexie crossed her arms, glaring at me.
"And you're being extremely mean. What's wrong
with you?"

"I just want this play to be as good as
possible."

"So do we."

"It doesn't look like it! No one's listening."

"They're doing the best they can."

"This is their best? We have to be perfect!"

"Lou. You've got to chill." Nakessa draped her arm around my shoulder.

I shrugged her arm off. "Chill? Impossible. If I chill, we'll suck even more than we already do."

Lexie gasped. "You think we suck?"

"Well, yeah. I do. Perfection doesn't just happen. No one's giving it their all."

"That's a lie. We are too."

"Well, maybe not everyone should be in my play."

Lexie tugged on her ear. "Maybe **I** don't want to be in **your** play anymore."

"What? No...Lexie!"

Lexie stomped past Sophia Wabash, through the colony of ants, and toward the school doors. My anger cooled with every one of Lexie's steps.

I turned to Nakessa. "I just want my play be as good as..."

"...possible." Nakessa finished my sentence. "It's also supposed to be fun."

"But I-I'm the director." My voice shook. "It's up to me to make sure it's perfect. It has to be..."

Nakessa didn't stay to let me explain. She ran after Lexie. Linking arms, they marched up the school steps and disappeared inside.

# Chapter 28

# Babies.
# Babies. Babies.

At home, I walked into an empty kitchen, my tummy rumbling for a snack that wasn't waiting. Paper paint swatches in every color of the rainbow covered the table. I picked up a strip of yellow shades. "Sun-rise Sur-prise," I murmured, reading the name below the brightest one.
The one below it was more orangey. "Saska-Saskach-Saskatch. Whatever." I dropped the strip onto the rest of the pile. "Mom!" I bellowed.

"Up here." Her voice was faint.

"Where?" I stomped up the stairs. For some

reason my anger flamed hotter with every step. "Where are you!?"

"In your room."

Mom stood by the window with a measuring tape. "I'm trying to see exactly how long the room is." She pulled the metal tab out from the square box. "Can you grab the end for me?"

"I guess."

"Pull it as you go to the far side of the room." I stood against one wall, holding the tape measure about shoulder height. Mom stepped toward the opposite wall, the tape whizzed out of its case.

"Why are you measuring my room?"

"For the cribs."

"The cribs? I have to share my room with two babies?" *Not fair!* "How will I get any writing done? Or sleep? Babies cry all the time."

Mom started laughing. "No, no. They'll get your room, and you'll move to Dad's study."

"What?" I dropped my end of the tape. It bounced on the carpet and the metal bent at a right angle. Dad's study was **re-pul-sive**. Which means it was big-time ugly. Like old-fashioned brown and orange ugly. My heart pounded in my chest.

"Oh, sweetheart." Mom came to me. "Don't look so sad. We'll give the room a full Louisa makeover. I brought home a ton of paint samples. You can pick whatever you like. And if we need to, we'll go back to the store for more. We have the whole day tomorrow to pick a color, since you don't have school because of the in-service."

"Oh—okay," I said, even though it wasn't. I didn't want to change rooms at all. This was my room.

"I promise it will be your dream room. The study's way bigger than this one. Dad and I need to be closer to the babies."

Dad's study was downstairs. All the way at the back of the house. I swallowed. "It's-it's j—"

Mom's hand flew to her mouth. Her eyes grew wide. All color drained from her face. She darted out of the room and down the hall. The bathroom door clicked shut. Babies called. Guess I had to wait. Again.

\* \* \*

Dad and I stood in the doorway of the dingy study. Mom stood on the frayed, brown plaid sofa that sat opposite Dad's desk.

"Careful Nadine," Dad said. "You shouldn't be up there."

"I'm fine. Now, just imagine instead of this ratty old pull-out couch, you have your bed from upstairs. Or we could get a loft bed. You've always wanted one, right?"

"Sure." I stuffed my hands in the back pockets of my jeans. "I guess."

"And of course, new carpet." Mom stepped onto the floor. "Don't just stand there you two. Come stand right in the middle of the room with me."

"Don't argue," Dad mock whispered. "She's gone into Karmic designer-mode."

"Funny. Very funny, Mr. Fitzhenry-O'Shaughnessy."

"I prefer clever, but funny will do."

Dad and I stood on either side of Mom. She wrapped her arms around our waists. "Now. Close your eyes. Let the feeling of the room embrace you."

I sighed. The thing with Mom is that when she goes all woo-woo like this, it's best just to go along with her. I closed my eyes, blocking out the ugly room.

"The room is embracing me...too...hard..." Dad said. "Can't...breathe."

I giggled. "Me...too."

"Knock it off, Paul, or I'll send you both to bed without supper. Ignore your father, Louisa. He's a terribly bad influence. Now. Keep your eyes closed. Imagine that this is your new room. Everything is just as you would like it. Freshly painted, in any color you want."

"Okay." I closed my eyes, trying hard to push thoughts of raggedy old sofas from my mind.

"What is the first color that pops into your mind?"

"Blue, but not just any blue. Turquoise—a soft turquoise. With white trim." A full picture of my new bedroom came to view in my imagination. "The furniture is all white, too. Fluffy throw pillows, and a cozy, soft blanket. Oh! And I don't want a loft bed, just a bigger bed. And a way bigger desk." Go big or go home. And since I was already home, big was my only option. Maybe I should ask Mom to paint me a Go Big or Go Home sign to hang above my new bed. My eyes popped open. The ugly room didn't look so bad anymore. "I guess it does have potential."

Dad tousled my hair. "Way to look on the bright side. There's nearly always a silver lining. Even with this tacky wood-panelled room. Now who wants my world-famous pizza for dinner?"

"Oh. No." Mom groaned and ran from the room. "Poor Mom."

"Yeah. Those babies are going to have a lot of explaining to do when they arrive." Dad laughed.

"Yup." I didn't laugh though, because I'd wanted to be a big sister for such a long time, and now it wasn't nearly as much fun as I'd expected.

"I guess it's just dinner for two, tonight," Dad said.

It was strange. I didn't know until that very

second how much you could miss someone who hadn't actually gone away. Mom was only in the other room, and I already missed how life used to be. When it was just us. The Three Musketeers.

I wished the babies would just go away.

\*　\*　\*

"It was great pizza, Dad. The best." I laid Pearl's head on my pillow, then slid under the covers.

"Why, thank you." He rolled the edge of the comforter back. "Sorry Mom's out of commission again."

"Growing two babies must be even harder than growing one."

"It is." He sat on the edge of the bed.

*What will happen once the twins are born? Will I ever spend time with Mom again?*

"Earth to Lou." Dad jiggled my shoulder.

"Ah, yeah. Sorry. Daydreaming." I rolled onto my side to face him.

"Before you drift off and do some actual dreaming, tell me about your day."

"It-it was…" I really didn't want to talk about it. "Fine." My lips began to quiver.

"Huh. You don't look like you had a fine day."

"Well, I did."

"Okay, Pearl. Louisa had a fine day." He poked

Pearl in the stomach. "Even though her eyes are shooting daggers at me, like she might murder me in my sleep. Guess, I'll keep one eye open tonight."

"Dad. Why do you always have to be so, so..."

"Funny? Amazing. Clever?"

"No!! You're so **annoying!** Just stop it!"

A tsunami of tears poured from my eyes.

"Oh, Louisa, I'm sorry."

"It was..." I sobbed. "...a hor-hor-horrible...day! And...I don't want to talk...about it!"

Dad lifted me, blankets, and all. He pulled me close and rocked back and forth. "It's okay, Little Bug. Get the tears all out. I'm so sorry. Sometimes I'm too silly. Cry as hard as you need to."

And I did. I cried until my eyes swelled nearly closed. My throat ached. I hadn't one last tear to shed.

"I got you," Dad murmured as my eyelids slowly closed.

What I really wanted was my dad **and** my mom.

# Chapter 29

# The Rain
# Before
# the Storm

Friday was the in-service, so there was no school. It rained. And rained and rained. Unfortunately, that didn't stop Mom from dragging me with her to run errands. We went to six boring stores. On the ride home, I ranked them from least to most boring:

**6.** 24 Hour Tires
**5.** Manuel's Meat Mart
**4.** Low-Cost Foods
**3.** Eco-Friendly Paint Supply Co.

**2.** Penny Pincher Dry Cleaners

And the grand finale of boredom...no drum roll needed. It was too sad for fanfare...

**1.** Fred's Upholstery

The only good thing about Friday was when Dad got home and we had leftover pizza. Mom had a salad. Unfortunately, the smell of tangy tomato sauce made her stomach flip-flop, so she ate in the living room by herself.

Mom went to bed at 7:00, right when we started our movie. It was her earliest bedtime yet. Dad was right. Those twins were going to have a lot of explaining to do when they arrived. Which, if I'm totally honest, I was beginning to dread. I knew they had to be born, but things had changed so much already. What would happen when there were two adorable babies in the house? Who'd want to tuck an always-messing-up ten-year-old into bed? Anyway, after Mom went to sleep, Dad and I watched *Lilo and Stitch*. At least we tried to. We both fell asleep before Lilo got snatched by the space aliens. The next thing I knew it was Saturday morning. That's when things went bad. Really, really bad.

# Chapter 30

# 9-1-1

**B**eeeeeep. **Beeeeeep. Beeeeeep.**

I bolted upright in bed. My hand clutched Pearl's soft arm.

The smoke alarm! I threw the covers off, leaping across the floor. "Get up! Get up!" I ran into the hallway, bolting into my parents' room. They weren't there. "Mom! Dad!"

I tore down the stairs. Sweet smoke hit me. My eyes stung. Dad was attempting pancakes again. Coughing I entered the kitchen. Mom had the window open, waving out smoke with a tea towel.

"Good morning," Dad said. He scraped burnt discs off the griddle into the trash can. "Third time's a charm. The next batch will be perfect."

He lowered a measuring cup into the flour bag. "Oh, no. We don't have enough. Maybe I should run to the store."

"No!" Mom and I said at the same time.

"Toast is fine with me," I said.

"Me too." Mom kissed him on the cheek. "I'll be back. I need to get out of these pajamas." She smiled at me before leaving the kitchen.

"Toast, huh?" Dad said.

"Yeah, it's safer. No offense."

He placed the griddle into the sink. Hot water sizzled as it hit the hot metal. "You know, I can't give up now. I feel I'm close to mastering pancakes."

I laughed.

"What? You don't believe me?" Dad tickled me in the ribs, with the dish scrubber.

"Dad!" I giggled. "Stop it. I'm going to—"

**Thump!**

"What was that?" Dad's hand jerked away.

We both looked up at the ceiling.

"Paul!" Mom's voice pierced the air.

Dad threw the scrubber into the sink and raced from the room. I followed close behind. I'd never seen Dad run that fast or take the stairs three at a time. Charging after him, I darted into their bedroom, nearly tripping over a stool on its side. Mom lay curled in a ball on the floor, clothes scattered all around her. Dad knelt next to her.

"I fell. I fell. Paul. The babies." I've never heard Mom sound so scared. Her face flushed, her eyes darted from her belly to Dad's face.

"Don't move." Dad looked up at me. "Louisa, pass me the phone."

I grabbed it from the bedside table.

Dad dialed three numbers. 9-1-1. "I need an ambulance. My wife fell and she's pregnant."

\* \* \*

I stood on the far side of my parents' bed, not wanting to get in the way. The paramedics slid a board under Mom, then lifted her onto a stretcher. Dad never let go of her hand until they wheeled her into the hall. I followed them down the stairs and out the front door.

*Please be okay. Please be okay. Please be okay.*

If anything happened to the babies, it would be all my fault. I had cursed them too! I was so dumb! Why did I make all those horrible wishes? First Mrs. Snyder and now Mom and the babies. My fists tightened and my nails dug deep into

185

my palms. Why had I wished Mom had never gotten pregnant? Nauseous guilt overcame me. I'd wished the babies would cease to exist. I had wished they'd go away. I was the **worst** almost-big-sister!

As they lifted Mom into the ambulance, she blew me a kiss. "I'll be okay, Louisa. Don't you worry."

My breath caught. She wouldn't be waving if she knew what I'd done. The twins deserved a better sister. If only I could be more like Lexie— who wasn't talking to me.

Dad stood next to me. We waved as the ambulance doors closed and pulled away from the curb. "Let's get inside, Louisa. I need to find someone to take care of you, so I can get to the hospital."

"Can't I come too?" I had to make amends somehow. Maybe I could find a way to stop the curse.

"I don't think that's a good idea. It'll be a long day. Not a lot of fun for a kid."

"I promise I won't get in the way."

Dad looked down the street, as the ambulance disappeared around the corner. "Uhm…okay. Fine. Pack your backpack with stuff to do. Mom's going to need all my attention."

"I'll be fast!"

# The U-nique Lou Fox

Dad pulled me in for a hug. "I sure wish my mom was here to help out."

I nearly said me too. But with all the wishing I'd done lately, everything had gone from bad to worse. Surely wishing for Grammers could only bring good luck, but just in case, I kept my mouth shut.

Dad pulled away. "Go upstairs, Get dressed. We need to leave as soon as possible."

"Right!"

I sprinted up the stairs two at a time. My hands shook as I changed out of pajamas, throwing on yesterday's clothes. I grabbed my backpack. My play binder was already inside. I grabbed the e-reader and headphones from my desk and scanned the room. *What else, what else, what—*

I stuffed Pearl into the bag.

# Chapter 31

# The Five
# Musketeers

**D**ad didn't say one word all the way to the hospital. I think we were driving too fast for him to speak. On the way, I slid Pearl out of my bag and clutched her tightly to my chest.

I closed my eyes. *Please be okay. Please be okay. Please be okay.*

We parked and ran toward the doors marked Emergency. Pearl flopped in my hand. I probably looked too old to have a stuffed animal, but I didn't care. I needed her.

Dad hurried to the front desk. "My wife came

in by ambulance." His voice shook. I'd never heard him sound scared before. My hands started to tremble.

The woman behind the desk tapped on a computer keyboard. "What's your wife's name?"

Dad ran a shaky hand through his bedhead hair. It stood out in thick clumps. He looked like a wild version of Dad. I hugged Pearl.

I closed my eyes, blocking out their conversation. *Please be okay. Please be okay. Please be okay.*

"Lou. Lou!" Dad shook my shoulders. My eyes popped open. Dad's eyes locked onto mine. "I need you to pay attention. You can't drift off now!"

"S-sorry, Dad. Sorry." My eyes filled with tears. I'd messed up again. I couldn't do anything right. I would never reverse the curse! I bit back a sob.

"Oh, Buggs. What am I doing?" Dad wrapped his arms around me. He lifted me up like I was a little kid again. I threw my arms around his neck, burying my face in his shoulder. Dad's voice was gentle when he spoke again. "I'm sorry, Lou. I was too harsh. Come on. Let's find Mom."

The woman smiled at us. "Teamwork. You'll get through this if you work together."

Just like The Three Musketeers, but better. The Five Musketeers. A whole new story—our story.

* * *

Mom had been taken to an area called triage. That's where they check your vital signs, which means making sure your heart and lungs are working okay. And if you're pregnant with twins, they make sure the babies' hearts are okay, too. When they let us see Mom, she was crying. I started crying too. So did Dad.

Dad stepped around the tubes that were attached to Mom's hand. "Is everything…"

"Yes. Well, mostly. The babies are perfectly fine."

Dad hugged her. My shoulders sagged. The twins were okay. My wish hadn't hurt them.

"I'm dehydrated," Mom explained. "Apparently, that's why I got dizzy and fell off the stool. Plus, pregnant ladies are more klutzy. I'd forgotten about that."

I sank down in a chair at the end of the bed. These babies had **so** much explaining to do. And I had a lot of thinking to do.

# Chapter 32

# Nothing Better Than a Double-crossed Heart

At bedtime Dad tucked Pearl in next to me as my head sank into the pillow. "So, Mom is for sure coming home from the hospital on Monday?"

"Hopefully." Dad picked up a sweatshirt from the floor and tossed it on my chair.

"I should stay home then. She's going to need help." There had to be a way I could make up for my wishes.

"Don't worry about her. I'll be home to make sure she follows the doctor's orders."

"Yeah, but I could help you both. I could teach

you how to make pancakes while Mom rests. In fact, I could stay home the whole week. No problem."

Dad sat on the bed and look directly into my eyes. "I am sensing there is another reason you don't want to go to school. Has something happened?"

"I-I did something. Something bad. A couple of bad things, actually." I buried my face in Pearl's snout. My voice muffled through her stuffing. "I don't want to talk about it."

"If it's making you dread school, I think you should tell me about those bad things."

What if Dad got mad at me too? Worse yet— what if he didn't think I'd be a good big sister anymore?

"Louisa." Dad's voice was soft. Gentle. "Is this why you were so sad on Thursday?"

"That's part of it." I pulled my face away from Pearl. "I kind of…exploded at everyone when we were practicing the play."

"Oh."

"Yeah, and Lexie's not talking to me." I spoke so quietly I could hardly hear my own voice. "She hates me."

"*Hmmm.* Do you really think that's true? You girls have been best friends since kindergarten."

I shrugged. "Maybe not anymore." Maybe I'd

made too many mistakes. Sharp twinges stabbed in my chest. Was that what a broken heart felt like?

"All I know is, if you hurt someone's feelings, you need to apologize. Even more importantly, you have to show them you're sorry. You can't just say it."

"I'll try." Show Lexie I was sorry. How was I going to do that? She wasn't even talking to me.

"Good. That's all you can do." Dad looked at me over his glasses and smiled. "Dr. Dad is in. Now, what else can I help you with?"

I tried to smile back, but my lips wouldn't listen to me. "It's bad. Really, really bad. Over a week ago, I did something, and I lied to you about it." Tears stinging, I blinked hard, staring up at the ceiling. It was easier to talk if I didn't have to look at him.

"Last week I told Mrs. Snyder I wished she was dead. She was being so mean. I thought she hated me, but I was wrong. Really wrong." Guilt made my words pick up speed. "Mrs. Muswagam told me on Thursday that all this time, Mrs. Snyder was actually trying to help me! She even arranged for some dyslexia doctor to come to school to speak to all the teachers at Friday's in-service."

"That's good. That means—"

"But Dad, Mrs. Snyder's been away sick! She's

probably going to die! And it's all my fault! If she dies—I'll be a **murderer!**" I hid my face under Pearl's once-plump body. All my loving attention had hugged most of her stuffing flat.

"What? Oh, Buggs. Calm down. I don't understand—how are you killing Mrs. Snyder? She seems a pretty tough lady. I mean, Shadow Phantoms would be very tricky to kill."

"My wishes! They turn into curses, and they come true."

Dad was silent. I glanced at him. His lips trembled. Then he started laughing. "That's really not how wishes work. Never, sweetie. "

"Dad, it's not funny." I closed my eyes and carried on spilling my guts. I needed to clear my guilty conscience. "I wished Mrs. Snyder would never come back to school. Then she got sick. Really sick. Kids are saying she probably has pneumonia. Sophia Wabash said old people die all the time from pneumonia."

"Hold on a second. Isn't Sophia Wabash the really tall girl in your—"

"Her mom's a nurse. Sophia Wabash knows everything about sickness."

"She's ten. She can't possibly—"

"Well, she **does!**" I glared at Dad. "And Grammers always says 'Be careful what you wish for.' So did Lexie—when she was still talking to me. Lexie also said it was bad luck to wish bad things on people."

"Buggs, we make our own luck by our own actions. Not by making wishes. Wishing bad things is unkind, not deadly."

I was very, very quiet. "What about Mom and the babies?"

He shook his head, shrugging. "What about them?"

I pulled my covers over my head. It was impossible to tell Dad how horrible I was when he kept looking at me with his kind eyes. "She's on bedrest because I wished she never got pregnant. I wished the babies would cease to exist. I **cursed** my own family. You should disown me."

"Lou. Mom's on bedrest because she's growing two mini-Louisas in her belly. And about the babies...I think you were just overwhelmed with jealousy. Adding two more people to our family is overwhelming for all of us. And jealousy is a very normal human emotion."

I peeked one eye out from under my comforter. "Really? You don't think I'm the worst big sister?"

"Never. And if I truly believed your wishes were magic, I'd get you to wish that your mom would be less stubborn and ask for help, instead of climbing on stools to put away laundry." Dad pulled my covers down. "And I'd get you to wish that we'd have a self-pancake-making-griddle, or would that be a self-making-pancake griddle?"

I giggled. "You're getting better at making them."

"No." Dad laughed. "I'm not. But you can't be good at everything."

"No, but messing up at school sure is tiring."

"I know spelling is difficult for you. I know math facts drift from your mind like smoke in the wind. I know focusing in class is like climbing a mountain backwards—with your eyes closed. These are all things we can work on together. But you, Bugaboo. You are a special, creative, loving, artistic, and compassionate girl. And you'll be the best sister the twins could ever have. So just focus on what makes you great. No need to change a thing."

"That's a relief, because my whole More-Lexie-Less-Lou plan failed."

"I'm sorry, More Lexie and Less Lou.... What does that mean?"

"Lexie never gets in trouble. Not even once since kindergarten. I thought if I was more like her and less like me, I wouldn't mess up so much. But it didn't work."

Dad stopped smiling. He turned very serious. Which isn't his normal MO. He pushed his glasses up his nose. I stayed very still.

"Louisa Elizabeth Fitzhenry-O'Shaughnessy.
No more of this More-Lexie-Less-Lou" business.
I don't ever, ever want you to be less Louisa. No
matter what. Do you understand?" Tears sparkled
in his eyes.

"Yes," I murmured. Tears formed in my eyes
too.

"Cross your heart?"

I crossed my heart. Twice. Dad crossed Pearl's
heart. My double-crossed heart could not have felt
any fuller. Unless Mom was there. And the babies.
Maybe I could cross their teensy hearts through
Mom's ever-expanding belly.

# Chapter 33

# Courage Needed

Dad walked me to school on Monday morning, which was comforting because I was nervous about seeing everyone. Especially Lexie.

"If all goes well, Mom will be home today," he said.

"I can't wait." I stopped, because an extremely awesome idea popped into my head. "We should get her one of those little brass bells. She can keep it beside her bed to ring whenever she needs anything. Like a queen—a mom queen."

"That's a super idea! I'll find one on the way to the hospital."

I slowed as we neared Lakeside. Kids piled off the two school buses parked at the curb up ahead. Shouting and laughing, they raced toward the schoolyard.

Dad leaned down and whispered in my ear. "You got this, Lou." He kissed the top of my head. "Mom and I will be waiting for you after school." Dad waved then hurried back down the street.

Staring at the school and all the other students, I exhaled. All I needed to do was show my friends how sorry I was. No biggie. My stomach flip-flopped. I crossed my heart, then crossed my fingers. I had to make this right. I raced around the side of the school.

*Please be at our tree. Please be at our tree. Please be—*

Lexie and Nakessa were not at our tree. In the history of ever, this had never happened. Even if one of them was sick, the other one would still be there. I scanned the field. Tons of kids, but not the Bendables. They weren't over at the stump maze or playing foursquare either. They were nowhere. My stomach soured.

How could I apologize if I couldn't even find my best friends?

I wandered over to the back steps. Maybe they were in the washroom. I darted up the stairs to the door. Cupping my hands to the window,

I peered in. That's when I saw her.

Mrs. Snyder!

*And she was not dead.*

I swung the heavy door open. Racing inside,
I ignored the kindergarten teacher who called to
me to stay outside until the bell rang. I had to talk
to Mrs. Snyder that very moment.

* * *

Mrs. Snyder disappeared into the classroom.
I ran after her. "Mrs. Snyder!" My words bellowed
through the room. "You're alive!"

Mrs. Snyder laughed. "Of course, I'm alive."

"It's just—I'm so happy to see you!" I stood just
inside the doorway.

"And I'm happy to see you too."

"I-I wanted to say something…" Suddenly my
hands went all clammy. "I wanted to—"

**Brrrriing!**

"Let's talk at recess. There's something I need
to discuss with you."

"Oh, okay." I tried to calm down. I mean, she
did arrange an entire teacher day to help me,
but she still seemed Shadow Phantomy to me.
I took a deep breath as I hurried to my desk, even
more anxious for Lexie and Nakessa to arrive.
My apology kept bubbling inside me. Like a sorry

volcano, I was ready to erupt with remorse. When my best friends entered the classroom, I waved. They both looked away. Lexie crossed her arms as she marched straight to her seat. Nakessa did the same. Both refused to look at me. My breath caught in my throat. I **im-plod-ed**. Which is possibly a ten-dollar word for saying, overcome with sadness. I collapsed and laid my head on my desk. Out the window our oak tree swayed. I closed my eyes and willed myself not to cry.

*  *  *

When the recess bell rang, I stayed in my seat. Everyone else raced from the room. Not one person had looked at me all morning.

"Louisa," Mrs. Snyder appeared at my side as silently as ever. "I'd like to talk to you." She sat down at Lexie's desk.

"At Friday's in-service, I learned all sorts of exciting ways to help you, that will benefit the whole class. I also learned that in my efforts to make sure you didn't fall behind, I made things harder for you. I need to apologize."

I sat up straight. I double-blinked at her, certain I had misheard my teacher.

"Will you forgive me?"

"I...I..." I didn't know what to say.

"You don't have to forgive me right away. Sometimes people need time to think things through. I do hope—"

"Yes! I forgive you."

"Louisa, you don't know what a relief that is to hear." Mrs. Snyder let out a long breath.

"The thing is..." I twisted my fingers together on my desk. "I have to apologize to you. I-I sort of..." I stared at my hands. Apologizing is not a walk in the park. Walks in the park are soothing— not if it's raining or hailing, of course. Probably one of the last places a person should be is in—

"Take your time, Louisa." Mrs. Snyder's words snapped me out of the park and back to my desk.

I shook my head. I'd drifted during my apology!

"Apologizing is like any other skill. With practice it gets easier." She laughed. "And when you reach my age, you're something of a professional."

I smiled. "I've been apologizing more than usual lately, so I bet I'll be a professional way before I'm as old as you."

Mrs. Snyder's eyes went wide. I thought they might pop off her face.

"I...I...oh, no." I couldn't even apologize without making things worse!

Mrs. Snyder removed her glasses and dabbed at her eyes. "Oh, Louisa. You are a breath of fresh air."

I shook my head. "Not always. Last week when

you were sick, I wished you would never come back. It was really, really mean. I'm so sorry."

Mrs. Snyder smiled right up into her eyes. They sparkled. "I accept your apology."

"Really? Just like that?"

"Yes. Just like that. Now, time you went out for recess."

"Right." I slowly stood. "Maybe I could help you in here." I looked around and pointed at the classroom library. "Those books could be tidied up."

"Stay inside on a beautiful fall day? Louisa, are you sick now?"

"No, I..."

Mrs. Snyder titled her head.

"I really messed up the play when you were away. I got totally bossy. I yelled at everyone. Lexie quit. Now, she won't speak to me. Nakessa won't either."

"I see. Time for another apology?"

"Yeah." I traced the edge of my desk with a finger. "I'm scared. What if no one forgives me?"

"Louisa, you can't make people forgive you." Mrs. Snyder reached over and squeezed my hand. "All you can do is speak from your heart and try hard not to repeat your mistakes."

"You make it sound easy."

Mrs. Snyder smiled. "It won't be easy, and it will take courage, but I think your friends are worth the effort. Good friends are too important to lose."

# Chapter 34

# Apology Gifted

I wanted to cross my fingers that the class still wanted to perform the play, but I was done with wishes and curses and anything else superstitious. Instead, I just hoped they would forgive me. When I saw the entire cast standing under our oak tree, watching me approach, I nearly turned around and ran back inside. I swallowed. I had to make this right. I had to apologize.

*Go big or go home.*

I needed to go bigger than big and more enormous than enormous. I needed to apologize to infinity.

Nakessa and Lexie's arms were linked. I ached for their friendship. Even if they never forgave me, I had to at least try. My friends were too important to lose.

"Hi, everyone." I said in a trembly voice. I needed to calm down. I took a slow and steady breath, as forty-eight eyeballs stared at me. Not one of them seemed happy to see me. Heat raced up my neck. "I-I owe all of you a huge apology."

"You sure do," Lexie muttered, tugging on her ear.

"I was really m-mean on...Thursday..." Panic filled me. A cold breeze swirled and the last few oak leaves drifted to the ground. What if my stage fright came back and made it impossible to continue my apology to infinity? I simply had to do this. "I was really mean on Thursday, and this play is supposed to be fun." Suddenly, Mrs. Snyder's words popped into my head. *Start the day as you mean to carry on. With your best foot forward.* "I hope you'll accept my apology, and that we can have a fresh start and enjoy ourselves." Lots of kids smiled at me. Sophia Wabash gave me a double thumbs-up.

I forced myself to look right at Big Jack. "I was

really, really mean to you, Big Jack. Will you accept my apology?"

He just nodded. He opened his mouth, but nothing came out. Instead, he smiled.

I smiled back at him. Last week I had called him dumb when he didn't know how to reply to me. I truly regretted that. Now to **show** him I was sorry I said, "Now, when you say your line, I'd like you to block the ghost from reaching Little Jack, who's the only student who isn't possessed. You save him and become a hero too."

"Woohoo!" Big Jack hooted. "I'm a hero."

Next, I turned to my best friends. "Lexie, Nakessa, I owe you both the biggest apology. This was **our** play. I never should've made changes without you. I should have listened more."

Nakessa smiled big. Lexie's hand dropped from her ear.

"I'm open to all your suggestions, or if you want..." Time to show the Bendables how truly sorry I was. "...I don't have to be the director anymore." My voice became whisper quiet. "Please don't stay mad at me forever."

Lexie untangled her arm from Nakessa's. A slow smile spread across her face. "How could we stay mad at you?"

"*Lou-ba doo, what would we do, without youuuu?*" Nakessa sang.

"Come on everybody," Lexie shouted. "We've got a play to rehearse!"

Apparently, I'm not only friend-gifted, but I'm apology-gifted as well. And if practice makes perfect, by the time I'm as ancient as Mrs. Snyder, I'll be a master of the apology.

# Chapter 35

# Monumental

I ran all the way home, not giving the slightest glance at Mr. Popovich's gnomes. They could've been disco dancing for all I cared. I charged up the front steps and bolted inside.

"Mom?" I called.

"Up here!" she answered from the bedroom.

If I could've, I would've cartwheeled up the stairs. I zipped into her room, sliding across the hardwood floors. "Mom!!"

"Lou!" Pillows propped Mom up in bed. A book on pregnancy lay face down across her belly.

"Can I hug you?" I glanced at her tummy. "I don't want to hurt you—or the babies."

"Of course, you can. Now get over here!"

"Mom, I missed you so much. You won't believe how much has happened!"

"I've only been gone two nights."

"It feels like a lot longer."

\*   \*   \*

For the rest of the evening, whenever Mom rang the little brass bell Dad had bought, I ran to take care of her. I even got to tuck her into bed, as if she was the kid! That night felt like a fresh start at being a big sister. This time, I was determined to start as I meant to go on. And start as one hundred percent Lou.

\*   \*   \*

Dad sat on the edge of my bed as I tucked Pearl under the covers next to me. "Good job tonight, Bugaboo. You took perfect care of Mom."

"I was practicing for the babies. I know I'm too young to babysit, but I can help Mom out loads. I can rock the twins to sleep. I can make up bedtime stories...act out plays...and when they get older, if they have trouble reading or printing or anything, I'll make sure they never feel bad about it."

"See? What did I tell you? Mom and I couldn't ask for a better big sister. But I do have one question." He looked at me all serious over the rim of his glasses. "Will you change diapers?"

"Ew."

I tried hard not to be totally grossed out. I failed, but if I was going to be the best big sister, I'd have to figure out a way to deal with stinky poop. Ick. "Maybe Lexie or Nakessa could give me a few lessons, before the babies are born."

Dad's eyes sparkled. Was he going to cry? "Those babies are so lucky." He pulled the covers up higher, right under my chin.

"What'll happen tomorrow? Who's going to take care of Mom while I'm at school and you're at work?"

"Don't worry about that. I'm sorting it all out." Dad yawned, tweaked Pearl's snout, and then kissed me on the forehead. "You need a good night's sleep. Tomorrow's your big day."

"Yes, it is."

In fact, it was **mon-u-men-tal**, which means extremely important. Fingers not crossed; I'd make Mrs. Snyder proud.

# Chapter 36

# Not Easy
# But Worth It

The rehearsal at lunch had a few bumps. Big Jack forgot his line again.

"I'm sorry," he said. "I'm more nervous than when I recited The Cub Scout Promise in front of my pack. I barfed on my cubmaster's shoes."

"Yuck." I thought of my stage fright. "I know what it's like to get so nervous it's hard to speak. Thankfully, I've never thrown up on anyone's feet."

"Yeah, but what about the play? What am I gonna do?"

"Good question." A few days earlier, I might

have asked myself, *What would Lexie do?* But instead, I thought about how making all the big decisions about the play had hurt my friends' feelings. Hurting my friends was not a very Louisa Elizabeth Fitzhenry-O'Shaughnessy thing to do. "Hey everyone," I called to the cast. "Who thinks Big Jack should say whatever pops into his head when he's onstage?"

Everyone raised their hands.

"Now you don't have to worry about remembering any lines. Just say anything at all. Okay?"

Big Jack's whole body relaxed, as he let out a long breath. "Okay, I can do that."

"I know you can, son." I drawled like Grammers. "I'm more certain of that than I am about the sun rising in the east every mornin'."

Big Jack blushed. "Uhm, thanks. I think. I'm just glad you're not mad at me anymore."

* * *

As we waited in the hallway outside the gym for our turn, my legs jellified. I grabbed Lexie's arm. "I think...I think I'm going to faint."

"Impossible. You're our fearless director!" Lexie did an extremely good impression of me.

I broke out laughing. Shaking out my arms,

I willed my nerves to settle down. "Okay, everyone. I want you—I mean—on behalf of Lexie, Nakessa, and myself, I'm hoping you all break a leg out there!"

"Break a leg?" Little Jack's voice rose two octaves. "Why would she want us to break our legs?"

"It's just a funny theater superstition," Sophia Wabash explained to him. "It's bad luck to wish someone good luck in the theater."

"Huh?" Big Jack grunted. "I don't get it."

"It's simple. No wishing going on here!" I laughed. "Only broken legs!"

Nakessa peeked through the crack between the gym doors. "Some second grader is juggling tomatoes! Two smashed onto the stage. Poor kid."

I slowly exhaled. One more act—another juggler—but this time a fourth-grade girl juggling four oranges. Then we were up. *Big time, here we come.*

\* \* \*

When our turn arrived, I stood in the middle of the stage with a classroom scene set up behind me. Students sat at desks on one side of the stage, pretending to be silently reading. The teacher's desk was on the other side of the stage.

I looked at the sea of faces staring back at me. Packed full of people, the gym looked huge from up here. Clearing my voice, I spoke into the microphone. "H-Hello, I-I'm Louisa and we-we..." my mouth dried.

*Oh, no!*

Not stage fright again. I glanced over at Nakessa and Lexie on the other side of the stage. They both gave me a double thumbs-up.

Swallowing, I looked across the audience. Mrs. Snyder stood at the back of the gym. She slowly nodded at me. This wasn't going to be easy, but it would be worth it. *I can do this.* "Our class would like to d-dedicate our play...to our teacher, Mrs. Snyder, who always gives second chances and who works hard for us every single day."

The cast started cheering. Mrs. Snyder's face went super red, and her smile? Even from up here, I could see it was **ra-di-ant**, a fancy way of saying it glowed.

"And...I'd also like to dedicate the ghost in our play to Nakessa's grandmother, Mrs. Kaur. Now, without further ado, I present *The Haunting at Lakeside School*."

# Chapter 37

# Fun. Better
# Than Perfect

I scurried to the side of the stage to stand beside the tomato juggler. "Good try with your act," I whispered.

He smiled. "Thanks, next time I'll use apples."

"**Woooooh!**" Nakessa moaned from offstage, out of sight of the audience. "Where are those **naaaasty** children?" She swooped onto the stage, her white sheet billowing behind her. "**Mwwwwahahahahaha!**"

Everyone leaped out of their desks, screaming and shouting, "Get away!" and "No!" They ad-libbed like professional actors. Running around desks, Nakessa chased them one by one off the stage.

As planned, only Little Jack remained, and he scurried under the teacher's desk. He peeked out from underneath and looked right at the audience. "Oh, no!" he cried. "The Ghost Principal Kaur Choo got all my friends!"

I shook my head. Little Jack wasn't supposed to speak to the audience. This wasn't that sort of play.

"What are we going to do?" Little Jack bellowed.

"Keep hiding!" A kindergartner shouted from the audience.

Giggles rippled through the gymnasium.

Little Jack disappeared under the desk as Lexie raced onto the stage. With her wand held high, she looked around the classroom. "I have to stop Principal Kaur Choo, before she possesses everyone in the school and turns them into ghosts, too!"

She raced offstage.

Shrouded in white bed sheets, the now possessed fifth graders drifted back into the scene, moaning, "**Wooooh. Wooooooh. Wooooooooooooh.**"

Then one ghost drifted herself right off the stage. "**Oooof.**"

"Ghost down!" said the juggling kid next to me.

"Sort of like your tomatoes," I muttered.

"I'm okay," the fallen ghost shouted as she crawled back onstage, joining the ghosts as Nakessa began to sing.

*"Lakeside school is haunted now,*
*haunted now,*
*haunted now.*
*Lakeside School is haunted now!*
*Look out! Or you'll be NEXT!"*

The entire ghost crew joined in for another verse before moaning their way offstage, just as Lexie appeared on the other side. Gripping her homemade Harry Potter wand, she tiptoed to center stage. "I can't do it alone. If only I had help. Someone the ghost wouldn't expect..." Lexie sat at a desk. "Hey, little ant." She pretended to pick something tiny off the desk. "Better go hide, or you'll be turned ghostly—wait! That's it!"

Lexie waved her wand in large swooping arcs above her head. "Hocus pocus, spell please focus. Make this ant understand me." Her voice grew louder as she spoke, in a perfectly magical way. "Please help me set everyone free!" She flicked her wand. *"Anto Helpo Presto!"*

Sophia Wabash leaped onto the stage. Dressed all in black, she had a sparkly, silver princess tiara wedged on her head between her

black pipe-cleaner antennas. "I'm the queen of
Lakeside School's ant colony, and we won't allow
any ghosts here!"

The ant colony scurried onstage, bumping
into each other as they lined up behind her. Their
antennas wobbled.

"Come on troops!" Sophia Wabash shouted.
"Let's show this ghost who's boss!" She broke into
song,

*"The ants came marching two by two, hurrah,
hurrah!*

*The ants came marching two by two,*
*to save the school from Mrs. Choo..."*

All the ants joined in, marching on the spot,
pumping their arms high. Their antennas kept
time.

Nakessa charged onstage.
**"Woooooooohhhhhh!** I'll get you too, Queeny!"
She reached for Sophia Wabash who tilted
her head to deflect Nakessa. The tiara caught
on Nakessa's ghost sheet. Snagged, Nakessa
jerked back, ripping the crown from Sophia
Wabash's head. The tiara flew toward the first
row of Kindergarteners. Mrs. Muswagam leaped
in its path, catching it in the nick of time.

Thankfully, Nakessa didn't get flustered. She
remembered her next line and swung around to
the teacher's desk. "I smell more fifth-graders!"

Little Jack scurried out from under the desk, screaming. "Someone help me!"

Big Jack raced across the stage and leapt in front of Little Jack, holding his custodian's toilet plunger high. "Get back from Big Bad Jack!"

Not even close to the line I had written.

The whole gym broke up laughing. Big Jack joined in. Also not in the script, but I couldn't help myself. I started laughing too.

Lexie shouted, "Principal Kaur Choo. Why are you doing this?"

"Because I failed a student. Long, long ago. Rebecca Le Croix was her name. She wouldn't listen. She never did her homework. I'm sure she never amounted to much."

"Rebecca Le Croix? She's my mother!" replied Lexie.

"Rebecca had children?"

"Yes, there's five of us."

"So, I didn't fail her. That means, that means..." Nakessa fluttered her arms to the sides, billowing her sheet. "I can stop haunting Lakeside School and journey to the great...**beyoooooond!**" She drifted across the stage and out of sight.

The remaining ghosts tore off their sheets, cheering. "We're free!"

Ants, students, Lexie, and Big Jack then began to sing.

*"Ding dong,*
*the ghost is gone,*
*the ghost is gone,*
*the ghost is gone,*
*ding dong, Kaur Choo is gone!"*

I ran onstage and shouted, "The end!"

The audience rose to their feet cheering. At the back of the room Mrs. Snyder wiped her eyes, then cupped her hands in front of her mouth. "Bravo!" she shouted.

The cast stood in two long rows and bowed. Lexie looked at me when they stood upright. "Come on, Lou Fox! Take a bow!"

I squeezed in between Nakessa and Lexie right in the center. We bowed. Then bowed again. My heart raced, but this time in the very best of ways. At that moment I felt like a real, live playwright. Mrs. Muswagam was right. We had needed an audience.

*   *   *

All the way home, I replayed every moment of the play. It certainty hadn't been a Broadway masterpiece. For sure it wouldn't be nominated for a Tony Award, but boy did we have fun. We're already planning a holiday play. So far, we've all decided there will be dreidels, Christmas trees, Chinese dragons, hoop dancers—and Little Jack wants a yeti.

As I turned down my street, I was so full of joy that I felt like skipping. But skipping in fifth grade is a lot like growling—socially unacceptable. Instead, I threw a cartwheel and followed it with a front walkover. Once I reached my front yard, I did a handspring onto the soft grass.

I bounded up the front steps, excited to tell Mom about the talent show. The very second I stepped inside, I heard the jingle of dog tags, and a familiar voice called my name from the kitchen. "Louisa!"

"Grammers!!" I zipped down the hallway, sliding across the kitchen floor.

There she was, standing by the sink with a tail-wagging Velma beside her. "We're here to take care of y'all!" She opened her arms. I raced into them. Grammers. The wish, I didn't dare to wish had come true.

# Chapter 38

# The Best
# Wish of All

Mom, Grammers, and I were dipping tofu chocolate-chip cookies in almond milk when Dad arrived home.

"Dad!" I raced to the front door. Velma was right at my heels. "Grammers is here! She's going to take care of Mom and help with the babies. She's even going to help me paint my new room."

He laughed as I pulled him toward the kitchen. He gave Grammers a big hug. "Thanks for coming, Mom. I wish Dad could be here too."

Grammers pulled back, wiping her eyes. "Your

father is smiling down on us. And there's no need for thank-yous. Family does for family. That's it, and that's all."

"Nadine, did you talk to Lou about the babies?" Dad asked, as he snagged a cookie.

"I thought we'd do it together." Mom took Dad's hand.

"The babies?" My heart thumped in my chest. "Is everything okay?"

"Of course, Bugsy." Dad smiled. "We have your very first big-sister job."

"Really? Okay."

"We'd like you to pick out their names," Mom said.

"Are you serious?" I put my cookie on the table.

"As long as it isn't d'Artagnan." Dad chuckled.

Mom frowned. "d'Ar—who?"

I laughed. "Just leave it with the big sister."

Velma pushed her snout under my hand. Her classic request for ear rubs. A low rumble began in her throat as I obliged. She tipped her head back and howled.

\* \* \*

That night, Mom, Dad, and Grammers tucked me in. Velma curled herself into a ball at the end of the bed.

"It's getting kind of squishy in here," Dad said, laughing. "Is there even room for poor Pearl?"

"Oh, hogwash." Grammers sat on the bed next to me. She kissed my nose. Then she kissed Pearl's snout. "There's always room for family."

Mom stood in the doorway with her arms folded over her tummy. "A playwright for a big sister. These babies are very lucky."

I bolted upright. "The babies! I have a list of names. It's on my desk. Can you pass it to me, Dad? But don't peek."

He handed me the sheet.

"These are my top twenty picks. I think we should vote. The babies need the best names, names that will get them started off right. You know, on their best foot forward." I laughed. "I guess I should say, on their best feet forward."

Cozy under my covers with Pearl, my chest radiated with warmth. **Ju-bi-la-tion**—a million-dollar word meaning complete joy—filled me. The babies were lucky, but I was even luckier. One day, I'd have a Broadway audience, but right now, my family was the best audience I could wish for.

"All right, here we go." I glanced at the names I'd picked. "How about Lexicon and Nakessor?"

Grammers' eyes got wide.

"After the Bendables," I explained. "My best friends—Lexie and Nakessa."

"Uhm..." Dad shrugged. "I..."

"So, that's a no?" I asked.

Mom started giggling. Grammers joined in, followed by Dad. Velma began to howl. We laughed until tears ran down our cheeks.

I was surrounded by love.

Some things would never change.

# The End

# Mom's Tofu Chocolate Chip Cookies

- 2 cups flour
- 1 teaspoon baking soda
- ¼ teaspoon salt
- 1 ¼ cup brown sugar
- ¾ cup vegan butter
- 1 teaspoon vanilla extract
- ⅓ cup soft tofu
- Chocolate chips—the more the merrier!

## Instructions:

1. Preheat oven to 375°F

2. Stir flour, baking soda, and salt together and set aside.

3. In a separate bowl, blend tofu until fluffy.

4. In a third bowl, whip butter and brown sugar until light and fluffy—about two minutes.

5. Whip in the tofu.

6. Slowly add the flour mixture.

7. Stir in the chocolate chips.

8. Dollop two-inch balls onto a parchment-lined cookie sheet.

Bake for ten minutes. They will seem not quite baked in the middle, but once cooled they'll be delicious.

# Acknowledgments

Writing is a solo activity, but the stories writers create can be made stronger with critique partners who give honest feedback. Thank you to Louise, Alice, Deb, and Candice for killing my darlings when I was too chicken to do so. And to my long-time writing group The Anitas, your friendship and support is a highlight in my writing life. I may have stopped writing a hundred times over without your gentle encouragement. Again, I thank McNally Robinson Booksellers for allowing The Anitas space to meet and critique each other's work. You are a pillar of Manitoba's writing community and I can't imagine a Winnipeg without you.

Finding a great publisher who shares your vision is like winning a cosmic lottery. Working with Pajama Press feels as if I've won the biggest lottery in the publishing world. Gail Winskill is a writer's dream publisher. She connects with the characters and stories she selects in a way that is deeply personal and it shows in Pajama Press's award-winning list. Early on, editor Erin Alladin gave me hope and a chance to revise and resubmit my manuscript. I'm so very grateful to Gail and Erin for their belief in Louisa and her story. A huge thank you to Kathryn Cole who shared her editing wisdom and answered my many questions, teaching me in the process how to see my work in a different way. Finally, to Peggy Collins who brought Louisa to life with her cover illustration. Lou Fox looks exactly as I imagined her to be.

To my dear friend Colleen Nelson: I need an entire page to fully express my gratitude not only for introducing me to Gail, but for your support and friendship from the very moment we met so many years ago. Our writing sessions with Maureen Fergus, i.e. wine and gripe nights, inspire me to continue writing.

# To my readers:

Louisa—a.k.a. Lou Fox—embodies all of us who struggle with our uniqueness. Being dyslexic or having ADHD can come with many gifts that are often overlooked because of the challenges they bring—especially when attending school. Please know that just like Louisa, you are enough just as you are. Being different isn't good or bad and those differences make us each beautifully unique—and unique is pretty darn great.

I continue to be challenged by forgetfulness, talking too much, and loads of daydreaming and zoning out, but I've learned quick tips and tricks that help me every single day. I would never wish away my ADHD, because it gives me many gifts like creativity, thinking outside the box, empathy, and an adventurous spirit. If I could have one wish granted, it would be that you embrace all that you are!

# What is Dyslexia?

According to the website *Made by Dyslexia*, it is "a genetic difference in an individual's ability to learn and process information" (www.madebydyslexia. org). They add that the one in five people who are affected by dyslexia often have challenges with reading, spelling and memorizing facts, which is why the way we test children in school puts them at such a disadvantage. However, people with dyslexia excel with communication skills, creative thinking, and problem solving.

The International Dyslexia Organization states that this learning disability "is characterized by difficulties with accurate and/or fluent word recognition and by poor spelling and decoding abilities" (dyslexiaida.org/definition-of-dyslexia). Because the brains of people with dyslexia don't recognize the patterns in language the way neurotypical people's brains do, they may struggle with reading comprehension. Reading less overall can also make it harder to learn facts and vocabulary.

# What is
# ADHD?

ADHD stands for attention deficit hyperactivity disorder. It affects children at home, at school, and in friendships. It also affects adults. According to the website *Kids Health*, "A person with ADHD has differences in brain development and brain activity that affect attention, the ability to sit still, and self-control" (**kidshealth.org/en/parents/adhd.html**).

*ADDitude* is a magazine that focuses on the experience of living with ADHD. In their article "Inside the ADHD Mind," they explain that ADHD is "a neurological disorder that impacts the parts of the brain that help us plan, focus on, and execute tasks" (**www.additudemag.com/ what-is-adhd-symptoms-causes-treatments**).

Most people are familiar with hyperactive ADHD, but some people experience inattentive ADHD, which makes it hard for them to focus or remember instructions. Some people have a mixture of both types.

ADHD is often harder to diagnose in girls and adults than in young boys. Luckily, as more research is conducted and more attention given to all sorts of neurological differences, our ability to understand, accept, and assist those who think differently grows. Here are some helpful resources:

Made by Dyslexia:
**www.madebydyslexia.org**

The Yale Center for Dyslexia & Creativity:
**dyslexia.yale.edu/resources/parents**

International Dyslexia Organization:
**dyslexiaida.org**

Dyslexia Canada:
**www.dyslexiacanada.org**

ADDitude Inside the ADHD Mind:
**www.additudemag.com/tag/download**

CHADD—Children and Adults with ADHD:
**chadd.org**

Attention Deficit Disorder Association:
**add.org**